# Love's Sacrifice

## Georgia Le Carre

This book is specially dedicated to
all those who have loved Lana and Blake.

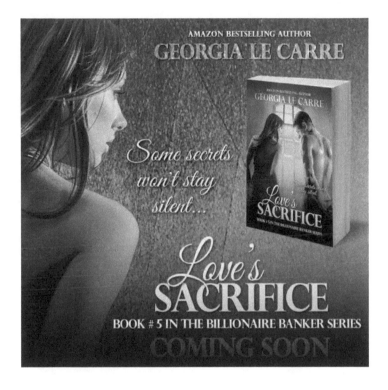

Editor: http://www.loriheaford.com/
Proofreader: http://nicolarhead.wix.com/proofreadingservices

ISBN: 978-0-9929969-5-6

You can discover more information about Georgia Le Carre
and future releases here.
https://www.facebook.com/georgia.lecarre
https://twitter.com/georgiaLeCarre
http://www.goodreads.com/GeorgiaLeCarre

This is your cup—the cup assigned to you from the beginning.
Nay, my child, I know how much of that dark drink is your own brew.

—Swami Vivekanander

# Contents

# One
## Victoria Jane Montgomery

I wake up in the dark, alone, cold...and restrained: leather belts on my ankles and wrists. My wrist shackles are so tight they are chaffing. I feel groggy and sick and quite frankly scared. I lift my head, look down and see that I am dressed in a hospital gown and robe.

My head throbs relentlessly, but I widen my eyes despite the blinding pain and cast them at the shadows and shapes around me. As my eyes become accustomed to the darkness I see that I am in a room, empty but for me and the bed I am lying in. There are no windows, only a large metal door with a covered peephole.

I listen intently. Not a single sound. Even my own breathing seems noiseless. Then: in the distance I hear the grate of a key in a metal lock. A woman wails down a corridor. The sound echoes eerily. A heavy door slams shut with a clanking sound and the impenetrable silence returns.

I cough. The sound is loud and unnatural in the bare coldness of my surroundings.

They have cut me away, their own daughter, and abandoned me here, in this mad house. Why did I not expect this? Why am I so surprised?

Because I'm NOT mad. There is darkness in my head, but my mind is bright and alive. Razor sharp.

'You're here for a rest,' the large, spectacularly ugly nurse said, when two orderlies hauled me into the hospital's reception area, kicking and screaming. She sounded conciliatory.

As an answer I bit her like a wild animal. Big mistake. She screamed like a banshee, they stuck a needle into my arm, and I lost that argument. My father stood back, staring, disbelief etched on his horrified face.

'Take me home, please,' I whispered to him before blackness came to take me. I guess he ignored my plea.

And now, here I am, in this cold functional cell. Angry tears gather in my eyes and flow down my temples and into my hair. The fury rages until it becomes a sickening, powerless sorrow. I wallow in it until a sound inside the room rouses me.

My senses on high alert, I jerk my head towards it. It seems to be coming from the left of me. It is too dark to see anything, but it sounds like the flapping of wings. Bats or birds. Adrenaline pumps through my body. Strapped down, I am easy prey for whatever is in the room with me. For the first time in my life I feel terrified. The temperature in the room drops suddenly and an inexplicable freezing cold descends upon me.

Utterly terrified, I begin to shiver violently.

I scream when my shackles are suddenly and miraculously loosened. Shocked, I pull my shaking

 2

limbs out of them and sit up. My heart is pounding so hard I can hear my blood roaring in my ears. For a moment I think my mind is playing tricks on me, but no—light is slowly filtering into the room, diluting the blackness.

My pupils are so widely dilated and my retinas so exposed by the blackness that I have to shield my eyes with my hands. The light is coming from what appears to be another entrance—one I had not noticed before. It is covered by floor length, thick red curtains. I drop my feet to the ground. The floor is ice cold, damp and clammy. I stand slowly. The room reeks of old metal. As if in a trance I walk towards the concealed entrance and draw the curtains back. I stand before antique, etched, leaded and stained glass doors. Through the glass I see a full, blood-red moon glowing in an unrelievedly black sky.

I experience no fear.

I push open the beautiful doors and enter a stone balcony. It is decorated with gothic friezes and gargoyles, and it is totally alien to, totally at odds with the bare, functional room I have been in. It almost feels as if I have stepped back in time or into a different dimension. The stone is freezing cold on my bare feet and the temperature is that of a winter night. My breath frosts in the wintery air, and yet I feel as warm as a sunned cat.

There is a sudden crash of thunder and the black sky splits open. As I watch, bright, shining light pours out of the crack. It turns into the shape of a very large bird that flies down. It lands on the

balustrade in front of me and becomes utterly motionless. Its silence and stillness are such that it is deathlike.

I gaze at it, this creature, this presence, with awe. It is the most splendid thing I have ever seen. Brilliantly colored and shimmering, its head is in profile so only one crimson eye is exposed to me. And all of a sudden, with a surge of joy, I understand: I am looking at the all-seeing eye. It is the great one Himself. El! He has taken the form of the phoenix that is on my family's coat of arms. He has come for me! I have not been deserted.

*You are Victoria Jane Montgomery.*

His voice reverberates *inside* my brain, piercing, intrusive and shocking. My hands shoot upward to grip either side of my head as I drop to my knees. I experience no pain as my kneecaps strike the stone floor. Only swallowed and possessed from within.

'Master,' I whisper from my prone position.

*Your bloodline and heritage are pristine and privileged... A gift.*

I turn my awed gaze up to the unblinking ruby stare that has seen it all. The ruby eye becomes darker and darker until it is a black hole that I am traveling inside. Thousands of years of the sublime and the profane open up to me like a blood-sodden flower.

The air leaves my lungs.

And ancient knowledge pours from the great bird like lava from a mountain. With it comes the knowing that this place will not contain me one

moment longer than I decree. This is not a place of purgatory, but a sanctuary where I may lay my plans and grow to unimaginable heights. I see now that I am the chosen one. My brother has been and always will be weak. I will be the head of the Montgomery dynasty. I will bring chaos. I have been chosen to do so.

Then the great bird opens its magnificent wings and flies away, and I am back in bed, restrained, my heart racing.

But transformed, illuminated and imaginably powerful.

I smile.

I am one of the chosen ones.

My only sin was to love and love too well. It was a mistake. I see that now. I wasted myself on him. Still, I have learned from it so it was a useful mistake. This place will not be the end of me. Never again will they stick a needle in me. I will affect submissive docility. I will beat them at their own game. I notice that they have cut my elegant nails to the quick. No matter. I will beat them at their own game. I am NOT mad. I don't belong within these walls. This is only the temporary seat of my power. From here I will destroy the man who tried to destroy me.

Blake Law Barrington—you thought you could put me out like trash, and someone would come along and remove me from your life... Foolish man. I know a secret, a secret so explosive that it will turn to dust the very foundations of the life you have built. I *will* have my revenge.

With a single, brutal blow I will bring you to your fucking knees.

# Two

## Lana Barrington

No matter what has happened. No matter what you have done. No matter what you will do. I will always love you. I swear it.

—*Defiance*, C. J. Redwine

He turns towards me. In the firelight he is impossibly chiseled, his eyes light and piercing, a hint of mystery about the corners of his mouth. We are on the first leg of our honeymoon, in the middle of the desert. Blake hired an old-fashioned camel caravan because he wanted us to mimic the ancient journeys of the silk road.

I stare at his beauty, memorizing it for the days when we will be old, feeble and sitting on a swing waiting for our grandchildren to come around, and they will be many.

'I want another child,' I tell him.

He reaches for me, his eyes suddenly dark and unfathomable. 'Not yet, Lana. We will have them, as many as you desire, boys and girls, but for a little while let me have you and Sorab to myself. I

have never been so happy. Just for a year I wish for nothing more than only the three of us. Our little family.'

I smile at him. 'One year?'

He nods, as hopeful as a child.

I laugh. 'OK.'

He pours tequila into two glasses. Shakes salt on the sides of our fists. It is strange drinking tequila in the desert. I look up at the night sky. Slow magic. The stars are shining like white-flamed candles in a pitch-black background, and there are so many shooting stars they seem to be raining down on us.

'Besides,' he adds. 'I want you to be able to do everything you ever wanted to, go where you haven't, see what you haven't, and experience it all. You will be pregnant when you're twenty-three, and four, and five, for as many times as you desire.'

'I only want three,' I protest with a laugh. And then my voice becomes serious. 'But I want to adopt a couple, too.'

He raises an enquiring eyebrow.

'I've always wanted to change a child's life,' I explain. 'To take it away from a situation where it could never prosper and give it everything I am able to.'

'The house is certainly big enough'.

'Thank you, my darling.' I lean forward and kiss him chastely on his cheek. My mouth lingers. He moves so it is his mouth on my cheek.

'The last time,' he says softly against my cheek, 'I missed everything. This time I want it all. I want to see your belly grow big with our child, your ankles swell up, and I want to be there when his or her head shows, and you are screaming blue murder. I want to wake up at ungodly hours and watch you feed them.'

'Stop, you're putting me off.'

He takes my hand gently. 'I'm so proud of you.'

The fire crackles. I move back and gaze at the hawk-like noses of the cameleers gathered around another fire a few yards away, to listen to an old man with a narrow, deeply wrinkled face tell stories. His voice is a hoarse whisper. The long sleeves of his gray tunic rise in a sweeping dramatic movement to point at some boulders in the distance. I wonder what tale he is weaving for them.

He strokes his beard, his eyes shining in the light, and the circle of men, squatting on their heels, lean forward eagerly, thrusting their heads out like lizards. I turn toward Blake. In the firelight he is watching me.

'Why?' I ask.

"When I saw you standing at the edge of the dance floor in your ruined dress, looking so lost and fragile, I felt like someone had stabbed me right in the heart. And yet you were more dignified and beautiful in your disgrace than any well-bred, stiff upper lip royalty.'

I shake my head; the memory is fresh and hurtful. 'No, I wasn't brave at all. I wanted to run

away. I was so embarrassed. I've never been so humiliated in all my life. All those people gawking at me, some secretly pleased, others pitying. I honestly thought our wedding was totally ruined.'

I press my fingers to his lips. 'But then you came and caught me up in your eyes and swept me into that dance. And suddenly, it was as if I was in a beautiful dream. I forgot everyone else— no one and nothing mattered, except you and me and our love for each other.'

'Because no one and nothing matters except you and me and Sorab.'

'And Billie and Jack,' I add impishly.

He remains serious. 'And all our other children when they come along.'

I take his serious tone. 'What's going to happen to her?'

He looks away from me, and stares unseeing into the leaping fire close to us. 'After you left with Billie I went to see her. I was so furious I wanted to kill her. I had to clench my hands into hard fists and hold them tight against my sides when I saw her, but almost instantly, I realized that something was very wrong with her. I had become an obsession. She was mad in a way I had never suspected. She didn't need to be punched, she needed psychiatric help. So I called her father and he agreed to commit her to an asylum.' He turns back to face me and looks deeply into my eyes. His voice is strong and edged with some deep emotion. 'She will never bother you again.'

'What about when she comes out?'

'She won't come out until she is diagnosed as well again. The tests she will have to pass are very rigorous and mean continuous observation over a long period. It will be impossible for her or anyone to fool the panel of psychiatrists. And I will be kept abreast of all her development.'

'That's good to know.' I pause. 'Blake, how safe is Sorab?'

He frowns. 'From her?'

'No, not from her. Just generally.'

'He is *very* safe. Why do you ask?'

'Even the president of America is not so safe that he can't be assassinated.'

'The president of America is assassinated if and when his controllers decide he is no longer a good puppet for them. Otherwise, he is impossible to assassinate.'

'My mother once told me a king is always killed by his courtiers.'

'That's true, too. Only they know the weakest spot to strike.'

'Who are your courtiers?'

'Why are you so afraid?'

'Because you are.'

He jerks his head in surprise, but I carry on.

'I feel your fear all the time. I feel it in the constant surveillance we are subjected to, in your voice, in your body. Who are we being protected from, Blake?'

'No one. I'm just a very thorough and cautious man. I don't trust anyone and I would rather be safe than sorry. Now tell me.' He smiles. 'Is this the kind of conversation a girl has with her husband on her honeymoon?'

I laugh. It's a nervous twitter, but it seems enough for him.

'What happened to the panties with the lacy bits and the new techniques from London, you little minx?'

I stand. 'Come into my tent in five minutes and I'll show you.' Then I turn and walk away, purposely swaying my hips in an exaggerated manner, so the robes swing tantalizingly around my body. At the tent entrance I turn to look at him. He is a silhouette, watching. And, for some reason, tense.

Slightly confused, I enter the tent, and stand for a moment behind the tent flap. I love Blake with all my heart, but his secrets are like a chasm between us. I get that he is trying to protect Sorab and me, but it pains me terribly to know that I have been deemed unsuitable to share his burdens.

For a moment, I close my eyes and give myself a talking to. *This is your honeymoon, Lana Barrington. Are you going to spoil it?* No, I'm not. I'm going to remember tonight as one of the best times of my life. I open my eyes and look anew at the magic that surrounds me. It is as if we have gone back in time. I note the wood stove, the cheap artificial carpets, the oil burning brass lamps, the antique wind-up gramophone, and the low bed, its orange silk sheets strewn with rose petals: our marriage bed. The smiling boy, Abdul, has done this.

It is a sweet touch.

The illusion is so perfect it is almost impossible to think that another world with Internet access, and automobiles, and TVs, and all manner of modern conveniences, exists. Strange, but I almost prefer this, this uncivilized existence. Meager and brutal, but real and honest.

Perhaps, in an odd sort of way, I have already nearly exhausted the trappings of wealth. I no longer care if my handbag has a Chanel logo on it. In fact, by a strange reversal I see the fake Chanel bag as the intelligent choice. The owners of the fake bags are the smart ones. They have understood a logic that the rest of us have been blinded to by clever marketing. Why pay seven thousand pounds for a bag you can get for twenty-five at the market? Especially since some of the fakes are so good the difference cannot be seen by the naked eye. A great con indeed.

My eyes return to the gramophone and my lips widen with pleasure. Blake remembered. I told him my grandfather had had one similar to this. I walk towards it. It is made of wood and it smells of lemon oil. I stroke the lovingly polished wood. I know exactly how to work it. Beside it there are new needles in a plastic bag. I take one out, and, carefully unscrewing the thumbscrew, insert the flat end of the needle into the hole. Cautiously, I screw it back on, as my grandfather stands over my left shoulder, saying in his gravelly voice, 'Be very, very careful, Azizam, the thumbscrew can be anywhere from sixty to a hundred years old.'

There is no one to call me *Azizam*, my dear, anymore.

With the new needle installed, I go through the selection of records beside the machine. Old Persian music. How thoughtful my husband is. I take a record out of its sleeve, dust it with the tip of my sleeve, and place it on the turntable. With a smile of anticipation—this is always the best bit—I turn the crank on the side of the machine until I feel resistance. With the main spring wound, I release the brake lever, and the turntable starts spinning. I lower the soundbox onto the smooth outer rim, gently push it, and watch it slide into the playing groove.

Crackling Persian music fills the tent.

My grandfather smiles as I sink down on some cushions. The air around me shimmers with memories. My mother is still alive. It is Norouz and all the children in the neighborhood are jumping over the fire for good luck. Old Behrouz, the sweet seller, brings sweets in a cloth bag. From his wrinkled mouth flow stories of heroic warriors from times gone by. There are all kinds of delicacies to eat and money to be had from the elders. But the memories are old and faded around the edges. They don't remain.

I stand, remove my long, thick robes and toss them on the carpet. They land, heavy, weighted with sweat and fine golden sand. I remove the expensive bits of underwear that I came to the desert with, and finding the long transparent blue veil I bought in the covered market, wrap it around my body and tie it over my breasts like a sarong.

There is only a small hand mirror with a carved silver back. I pull it down my body to see what I look like. My flesh looks pale, my nipples are twin peaks, and my belly button is a dark, round shape. I hear a rustle outside and moving to the middle pole drape myself around it.

The tent flap opens.

# *Three*

A cold gust of wind redolent with the smell of spit-roasted mutton scatters goose bumps on my naked flesh and makes the open flames dance. Blake stands stooped at the entrance. His gaze, smoky with alcohol, ignites, and his breath comes out in a hiss. He had not expected such a gift.

Whatever tension had lurked in his eyes while we were out there is no longer. Now they shine like gems in the yellow light cast by the lamps and candles. He doesn't say anything. Simply comes to within a foot of me, and stares: a hot, slow gaze. He seems different. He seems almost astonished... Maybe I am different too. His eyes meet mine, enchanting me with their magic, filling me with desert lust.

He reaches out a hand towards the veil, but I swirl away, nimble and light as an air sprite, and stretching my hands high over my head, I dance. The pulsating drums move my bare feet as I snake my body around the wailing music. I drag my hands up my thighs, my hips, up to my waist, and higher still, until they reach my breasts. Impulsively I pinch my nipples.

His eyes flare. Heat flushes in my belly. My nipples feel raw and my sex is swollen so thick I feel the lips rub sinuously against each other: maddening me. I look at him sensuously, with half-closed, come-hither eyes.

He responds to my silent call. He moves fast and is suddenly so close by, his deep voice vibrates inside my head. 'Who owns this glorious creature?'

'The one who dares...' I suggest, my voice trailing away wickedly. Like the honey you leave as a trap for the unwary.

'I dare,' he whispers.

I pull the veil over my face so only my eyes are visible and, turning from the neck, look up at him. 'Are you sure?' I ask saucily.

An intrigued eyebrow lifts. 'You should come with a warning, a bit like the cigarette manufacturers are forced to have on their packaging: Beware, scintillating to the point of incendiary.'

For some seconds I look at him. Outside miles of nothing, here, let there be swollen heat. I spread my legs and plunge my fingers into my wet folds. The action is primitive, perhaps even obscene, but here we are different animals. I thrust my fingers in and out, my breath becoming more ragged.

He takes off his thick robes and flings them to the floor, his eyes never leaving me. I see the smooth golden skin where his collar falls open. How beautiful is my lover. He pulls at the white shirt-dress. It joins the robe. Naked to the hips he comes forward, sexual energy rising off his glistening muscles like a heat haze. I gaze at his body. So familiar and so dear, and still the air zaps with my desire for it.

He catches my hand in his and brings it to his mouth. A smile curves my lips. I lean forward, my bare breasts brushing his torso as I sway with the music. It is like rubbing a magic lamp. It awakens a genie of dark excitement deep within his body. I see the fever-thirst come into his eyes. I stop smiling.

He spreads his fingers on my hips. They are like flames on my skin. I turn and let my shoulders rub against his chest, and my buttocks brush the hard flesh between his legs. His reaction is intoxicating—he reels me in suddenly so the base of my side is pressed into the rod of hot flesh. My limbs tremble in anticipation. He moves his body against me: long thighs, muscles, sinew, tendon and bones, all melds with me.

In response, I move my buttocks away from his body and slide my hand between us. I palm his hardness and curl my hand possessively around the hard shaft. It responds by twitching and growing harder still.

'Impressive,' I whisper.

He chuckles, a dark, possessive sound. 'The better to fuck you with.'

His hands roam my body, from my belly up to my breasts and down between my legs.

'Oh yes,' I gasp, gently stroking the bulge, wanting the brutal force of his thrusts and the agonized sound of my name on his lips as he floods me with hot cum. He bends his head and his mouth scorches mine, hot and hungry, the taste of salt and tequila, a sparkling shock. My eyelids flutter closed. We are ravenous creatures in the desert. He lifts his head, breath coming fast and shallow.

'If you don't get inside me soon I'm going to melt.'

As if on cue the music changes. The air fills with drums.

He wraps his thick and sinewy arms around me and, sweeping me off my feet, swirls me around so fast I am a dizzy blue mist landing on the orange silk bed. My weight crushes the flower petals. In dying they gasp out their sweetest scents. They mix with the oily scent of the candles.

He kneels down. His scent is different: he is as fragrant as the hot sand. He catches my eyes, smiles faintly and, parting my trembling thighs, sinks his fingers into me. My flesh flowers around the heat of his fingers. Grasping his hand, I hold his fingers deep inside me. I close my eyes and savor the delicious sensation of my muscles jerking and quivering around him, as they anticipate release.

My hands fall away as his fingers curl inside me and begin to stroke slowly. He knows exactly where to rub to make me explode.

'God! I'm so crazy about you,' he rasps, as his mouth descends on a nipple. Hot and rough. It burns me. He sucks the other deep in his mouth. Pleasure shoots straight into my sex, making more blood rush to it, swelling it further, until it...hurts. I whimper.

He stops and looks at me with heavy-lidded eyes.

'Don't stop,' I whisper hoarsely. 'Take me as if I am a captive you bought in a market.'

His smile drips with dominance and lust. 'What kind of a captive would you be?'

'What if I am an enchanted slave who is spellbound to her owner by dark magical cravings she can't resist?'

'A bewitched slave who can't say no. My, my... Must be my lucky day.'

I moan as his fingers pierce me hard and fast.

'I love watching you helpless and writhing at the end of my hand.'

I arch helplessly.

'And I own every inch of this purchase.'

'Every inch,' I croak. I grab his silken hair and pull his mouth down.

'So you want to be taken as a market slave, hmm?' His voice is dangerously soft.

'Yes,' I say, still only frustratingly impaled on his fingers.

Hands of steel flip me over so suddenly I yelp with surprise. With my head buried in the cushions I hear the sounds of his clothes falling away. My hips are grabbed and jerked upwards and held up tilted at an angle. When his cock slams into me I am still hazily aware of the men outside, so I scream into the pillow.

'This is what you wanted?'

'Yes.'

'And this?' He plunges in so punishingly hard I break out in a sweat.

'Yes,' I growl, like an animal possessed.

He goes at it, wild. Our mating is crazed and brutal. I bite the pillow to keep from crying out too loud. He grasps my hair and pulls away the pillow.

'Fuck you,' I snarl.

And he slams again into me. He pulls my ass cheeks apart and pushes deeper in. His dick feels hot, burning hot. I am already so sore and battered, my body is beginning to quiver, but just as I think I can bear it no more, I become aware that he is almost cresting. I know him so well I can feel it come into his body. I push my flesh against his groin and squeeze my muscles tightly together, and he groans and calls my name as he spurts and jerks into me.

For a few seconds neither of us moves. Holding me close against his body, he lays me back down on the bed, and rests on top of me, his shaft still buried deep inside me. I love the feeling of his weight on me, while he is half supported by his elbows. His lips settle on the pulse at the side of my neck. His tongue darts out to lick it. Then he puts his mouth on it and sucks it. A whimper escapes. He leaves the pulse and trails upward along the side of my neck to my ear. He nibbles the lobe.

'Don't stop,' I moan. My voice sounds almost anguished.

He pulls out of me and, rising to his hands and knees, turns me over. He straddles my thighs, holding my hands high over my head, and looks at my exposed body. His eyes rove over my body jealously. Then he lowers his head in a kiss so soft and sweet that it brings tears to my eyes.

'Blake?'

'Don't speak. I think I need to have my way with you,' he purrs.

My breath catches at the raw heat in his eyes, even though I am not sure I can take another pounding quite so soon. 'I thought you just did,' I say softly.

He smiles wolfishly. 'See what happens when you pretend to be a little slave girl?'

'Did I say I couldn't take another round?'

'That's true.'

He slides off me. 'Lift your legs up, knees straight.'

'Why?'

'Humor me.'

He grabs my thighs and opens my legs into a V. And then he takes his wolfish grin between my legs and devours me greedily. Literally consumes me. It just goes on and on and on until the climax comes with such shattering impact that it feels as if the back of my head has been blown off. When it is over I am sobbing with the intensity of the experience.

He gathers me in his arms until my heart rate slows, my breathing returns to normal and the crazy heartbeat stops.

'I think I could grow used to being a captive slave,' I say, encircling his neck and pulling his mouth down to mine. It feels so good to have his naked body over mine. I kiss him. He tastes of me.

'You really are the sexiest sheik that ever walked a desert.' My voice sounds soft and fluttery.

A corner of his mouth lifts. 'And you, my love, are the most beautiful slave that ever graced any tent.'

'What if I buy you in at the market tomorrow?'

'Honestly, can't wait,' he says, and his voice is so rich and deep my breath catches in my throat. For the rest of my life, no matter how long I live, I know I'll never forget this moment. The feel of his skin on mine, the handsome curve of his lips, the lock of hair falling forward and the look in his eyes. God, I love this man so much I would fight for him. Never again will I run away.

'Do you think the men outside heard us?' I murmur contentedly.

'If they didn't hear us before they will now,' he says, and, throwing a long, muscular arm gleaming with a sheen of sweat out, reaches for the jar of spreadable chocolate.

I giggle...but not for long.

# *Four*

$S$ometime during the night I awaken and, extricating myself from Blake's embrace, silently leave the tent. Outside in the white moonlight men smelling of camel are on night watch. They are boiling tea, or cutting their fingernails with the sharpened jawbones of animals, or making camel hair rope while they look out for hyenas. Hyenas, they claim, will even eat the dates from their supplies.

Out of kindness and respect they never look directly at me, but I am very curious about them. Through the interpreter, I am always eavesdropping on their conversations. They speak of the desert as if it is a woman—wild, unforgiving, mysterious, magnificent... In their blood. They beseech the clouds above to rain on their woman. 'Why not burst a moment here?' they entreat poetically.

Wrapped in thick blankets I sit apart from them in the icy cold and watch the moon, the whitest, roundest melon. It is still dark and utterly silent when the camel drivers begin to stir and greet each other good morning. It is a surprisingly long process. Again and again they ask each other, 'Are you all right?'

'Yes, I am. What about you?'

'I'm fine. You sure you're all right, though?'

'Yes, yes, I'm good. Really, are you?'

'Me, I'm fine. You are OK too?'

It seems they never tire of repeating the process at every dawn. No one looks at me as I slip between the camels huddled together, their backs white with snow and pieces of mud and ice stuck to the strips of cloth tied to their footpads.

Lizards are drinking the condensation off the frosted sand, when I lift our tent flap. It is lovely and warm, but too dark to see. I pause to allow my eyes to adjust, but I still manage to trip on the carpet's edge. A small sound escapes me and Blake whips his head around to look at me. It never ceases to surprise me how quickly alert and watchful his eyes can become. A stranger's eyes.

'Where have you been?'

'Watching the moon.'

'Without me?'

'I didn't want to wake you,' I say, coming closer. I light a lamp.

He sits up and the light oils his back so it gleams bronze. I sit next to him and run a cold finger down the bronze back. He shivers.

'Next time I'll wake you,' I say, and grasping his hair, tug it with me as I fall backward into the rumpled silk sheets. He lets me pull him down until he is only inches from my face, and then he stills and turns to look at me. His eyes are

unreadable—wet leaves in summer. I stare into the wet leaves. Part the leaves, Lana—behind them is the man.

'Lie back, husband of mine,' I say softly, sitting up.

He obeys and I hold my hands over the heat of the lamp. Then I pour heavily musk-scented oil into the palm of my hand and rub the two together. Warming the oil, oiling the skin. Very gently, I take his hand in my upturned one.

He whispers in wonder, 'It never fails to amaze me how such a tiny hand can make me feel so vulnerable and exposed. How odd that a giant like me should be undone by such a simple thing!'

I stare at him in surprise, and then I lie him on his front, straddle his buttocks and laying both palms on the small of his back take the first long sweeping stroke.

Afterwards, we eat bowls of gruel and drink goat's milk covered with a film of ice. He talks and I listen, bowl suspended between lip and floor. He is not soft. He cannot be soft. He wants me to know that. He has thrived on sharp arrows whizzing past his head, slicing his ears.

'I don't care,' I interrupt suddenly.

We are still whispering when the sky brightens. It is time to be gone. Outside the men burden the animals once more. And as they do, every time, the poor things snarl, groan, and protest.

Blake helps me onto the camel's back, and I am borne up. Perched high atop the animal, its

disdainful, hairy head swaying from side to side, its large eyes rolling, we resume our journey. The sensation is like being a tick on a gold beast. Hanging fast. Unwelcome.

A little while into the desert, and the cameleers start singing to their animals, their lusty, deep voices carrying far into the dunes. Each line the length of a man's breath, and each breath the length of a camel's stride. The songs turn that ocean of heat, sand and blinding light into a dream, hypnotizing both man and camel so they become one graceful creature.

Hour after hour we head east, rocking in the unbearable, scorching heat, mouth tightly shut against the sand in the wind, not stopping even to eat, only to pray. When the camel drivers, burnt and glorious, stop to pray, I want to lie down on the sand, but Blake, his face wrapped in a blue and white cloth against the burning wind, so only his eyes remain as cerulean as the sky, will not let me.

'You will only collect more heat from the ground.' He holds out a water skin. 'Drink, drink. In this heat one must drink—little but often—to be well.'

There is a sediment of black dust, but the water is cool. And in the desert water never tastes bad. Everyone drinks noisily, exhales noisily. I sip the discolored water, eat millet, dates and goat's cheese and wish for a gust of wind, but when it comes, it is a fiery blast that sears my lungs.

Queasy, dizzy, my vision ill with the glare and the bending waves of heat, we persist. What a strange place the desert! The emptiness of it. Indescribable. Animal droppings dried to ash in hours. Where there is grass it is scorched white. And yet I find it incredibly beautiful, and the experience unforgettable. Finally, the camels' bells stop, and Blake reaches up and takes me into his arms.

On foot, I watch the sun become red and the air orange. The temperature drops quickly. Darkness falls even faster. The men set up camp and water their animals. Fires are lit. Men crouch over their flames, blowing. The fires become beautiful orange flowers.

'Ain't you gonna wash me? I'm dirtier than a sweat hog,' Blake teases.

I grin at him.

Water is precious. We wash each other with wrung out washcloths.

When we come out of our tent, hours later, the men are huddled around the fire eating a sort of mutton stew, olive bread cooked on hot stones, and drinking date spirit. Abdul brings us our food on lovely blue glass plates. Hard to imagine they have saved these pretty pieces just for us. Such beautiful manners, these wild desert travelers. I smile my thanks.

'The desert mushrooms,' the interpreter tells us in his distinctly mannered accent, bowing his head politely, 'are for later. Desert luxuries.'

I nod. There is a world of difference between him and the cameleers. He is sly and gallant, and they are as noble and heroic as warhorses.

I work the tough, fatty chunks of meat with my teeth while I watch the warhorses enthusiastically lick their fingers, their wooden plates. Afterwards Abdul brings us delicately perfumed tea in dainty gold-rimmed glasses.

The desert makes no sound unless we make it. And so the men make their sounds, they chant their holy invocations to their God. The resonating sounds become part of the timeless desert landscape. I imagine the sound moving through the endless expanses of sand. Where does it go? Who catches it eventually?

It is when we stop for morning prayers the next day that the radio message comes through. At first I don't bother to listen, but the immediate stiffening of Blake's body alerts me. I turn to watch him curiously. The hardening of his eyes, the thinning of his mouth as he listens... Until he is a stranger.

'No,' he says finally. 'Give me two minutes then call me back.' He meets my eyes.

'What is it?' I whisper, my feet shifting nervously from side to side on the burning sand, my heart thudding in my chest.

'My mother is in Bangkok.'

Whatever I had expected, I had not expected that. I pull my hand away from my mouth, and, baffled, demand, 'Why?'

'She wants to meet Sorab.'

I shake my head in disbelief. 'Without us being there?'

'You decide. We can either stay and keep to the schedule or we can leave today.'

I don't have to think. Even if he had stiffened and become hard and cold I would not have trusted my son with her. His family give me the creeps. I want to leave at that very moment. 'Can we leave now, please?'

To his eternal credit he does not attempt to talk me out of my decision or placate me. Simply nods and lapses into a tense, thinking silence. When the radio goes again, he says, 'Arrange for us to be picked up now.' He pauses and I hear him say. 'Really?... Good.'

'What was that about?'

'My mother cornered Billie and insisted she be allowed to spend time with Sorab.'

'Oh yeah? What did Billie say?'

'Told my dear mother to fuck off.' He smiles reluctantly.

We wait for the helicopter in the glare of the sun in our city clothes.

'What will happen to the men?'

'They will return to their homes.'

In twenty minutes our ride creates a veritable sandstorm as it lands. Abdul kisses my hand and the cameleers turn to stare me in the eye for the first time. I am no longer a woman, but a curiosity. A woman who would bare her hair, the shape of her body, and her legs. Their eyes are like the desert. Timeless and full of secrets. I commit them to memory, knowing we will never meet again.

# Five
## Victoria Jane Montgomery

When the lunch bell rings I make my way to the canteen. Despite the restraints of that first night, it is not like *One Flew Over the Cuckoo's Nest* here.

In fact the first day was relatively simple Once they established to their satisfaction that temperature, pulse, blood pressure, EKG and blood values were all normal, and I did not harbor a desire to hurt myself or anyone else, they let me loose upon their premises and their 'experts'.

The experts' job is to get to 'know' me through lengthy interviews to excavate my full life history, my family background, and my criminal and psychiatric history. The assessments include personality tests, neuropsychological tests, tests for malingering (the technical term for faking a mental illness) and general cognitive tests from intelligence to memory.

You see, here, they believe in progressive and compassionate care.

The building I am imprisoned in is incredibly beautiful. It was erected in the nineteenth century by a baron for his mad wife. The interior is high ceilinged, and ornate, with long, rambling, sunlit wings. Apparently his wife had loved playing the piano so he had a grand piano installed in every room. After the servants found him stabbed to death—his face gruesomely contorted with horror—while she sat calmly playing the piano, the building was closed and abandoned for many years.

Now the ceilings are still full of intricate moldings to rival the Baccarat Gallery Museum in Paris, and the walls retain their original warm pinkish shade of off-white, but the pianos are gone, the windows have bars over them, and the sun-filled corridors are populated by over-medicated, dazed patients shuffling aimlessly up and down them.

And the large room where the Baroness played to her audience of one corpse has been designated the common room. It is dimly lit: the curtains remain drawn at all times. A huge television is mounted on one wall and patients wander in and slump in armchairs and rocking chairs to stare numbly at the flickering screen: cartoons playing on a loop.

I avoid it like the plague.

The dining area is full of natural light and rather pleasant, other than the unidentified brown smears and stains on the walls. There are no decorations except for a poster listing banned items—nail clippers, razors, tweezers, lighters, medication, belts, shoelaces, spiral-bound notebooks, jewelry and under-wired bras.

Of course, there are other things that are not on the poster that are banned too, like physical contact with other patients, food in the rooms. The only rule that concerns me is inpatients not being allowed to make calls, only to receive them. But I think I have the solution. She walked into my room this morning, keys jangling on her belt. The name tag pinned on her uniform, appropriately enough, said 'Angel'.

I walk along the aisle and a large, dozy cow in a blue apron slaps a huge mound of macaroni cheese on my tray. I stare at the thick, lumpy concoction with a sort of culture shock. This is what passes for food. Another uniformed staff in a hairnet dishes out the vegetables: green beans, carrots and a graying sludge that she calls mashed potato. I thank her politely, and, moving along, pick a bun from a basket of bread rolls. These would come in handy in Palestine when those kids run out of rocks and stones to throw.

Dessert is a wedge of something brown and crusty that they daringly pass off as chocolate fudge cake. Only the truly mad can eat it. I pass by the drinks dispenser and fill my Styrofoam cup with chilled fizzy orange and pick up some cutlery, plastic obviously.

With my tray of exciting cuisine I make for a table that is empty, and sit down. On the next table a woman in a white gown is drooling into her food. She looks like a zombie. I turn away from the sight with a flash of anger, at what they have done to me. I don't belong here. I shouldn't be here.

My eyes collide with another's—a woman at another table who stares at me murderously. My first reaction is to walk up to her and slap her hard in her face, but, of course, that would be contrary to what is expected of a model patient. I pick up my plastic knife and, never taking my eyes off her, slowly lick the plastic blade. She flinches and averts her eyes. That's bullies for you. Always cowardly in the face of true power.

I fork the 'food' into my mouth. It is horrendous, but I have already learned that those who don't eat are put on special watch. My plastic knife slices through the overcooked carrot. I spear it, slip it between my lips and swallow the watery mush.

A woman comes and perches timidly on the empty chair beside me. I turn and look at her. She has a wild, haunted look about her startlingly large, light eyes. I sigh inwardly.

'Be very careful,' she warns in a frightened whisper. 'There are spirits in this place. They are restless in their misery and waiting to attach themselves to humans.'

'Thanks for the warning,' I say, and turn resolutely away.

She floats away, a ghost herself.

'Everybody's curious about you,' someone says from the left of me. I look up. She is young, terribly common obviously, but not chronically mad. Probably just depressed or something. Her clothes are terrifically unfashionable, but her fingernails are beautifully done in baby blue. Hmm... They didn't cut her fingernails, which means she must be a model patient. She plonks herself in the chair vacated by the ghost.

'Are you really a lady? Most of the people who call themselves lord or lady around here are just barmy?'

'Hmm.'

'Cooool,' she crows brightly. 'I've never met a real lady before. It's sooooo boring in here.' She quickly makes herself more comfortable in the chair.

Inwardly, I am seething at the indignities I am being subjected to, but I smile politely and take a sip of the awful coffee. I never imagined coffee could taste so bad.

A man marches up to me. He is wearing a brown sweater and golfing trousers and his cheeks are so red it looks as though he is about to have a heart attack at any time.

'Why are you here?' he demands in a loud voice, his cheeks flushing even brighter red.

'I'm minding my own business. You should do the same,' I tell him.

Apparently that is the right answer. He nods as if impressed and walks away.

'Way to go, girl,' my unwelcome companion approves.

I turn towards her. She holds her hand out. Her nails, beautifully manicured, strike me as the most civilized thing in that place. 'Welcome to the mad

35

house. It's a treat to find someone who has the guts not to be floating around on their mind-fuck pills all day. I'm Molly Moss, by the way.'

# Six
## Lana Barrington

We fly into Thailand in the afternoon heat. Thailand, let me tell you, is not just hot, it is like a giant sauna. The humidity is such that my clothes start sticking to me during the short walk from the plane to the air-conditioned airport. In the car, I realize that I am nervous, and as soon as we arrive at the Banyan Tree, I leave Blake to check in and go up to our suite, while I make my way up to Billie's room.

'Hey,' she says, quite nicely brown and grinning.

At the sight of her relaxed, happy face, my tension fades. I was just being overdramatic and paranoid. Maybe it was being in the desert, where it did not feel like we were only a few hours away, but as if we had traveled back in time or to a different world.

Billie throws her arms around me. 'Sorry I ruined your monumentally epic fucks, but am I fucking glad to see you.'

I grin. 'So am I. So glad to see you. Look at you. You're already as brown as a berry.'

'Zero SPF always does the trick. Come on in,' she invites, and closes the door.

'Where is he?'

'Having his beauty nap. Jerry has gone to one of the hotel's gourmet cooking classes,' she explains, as she takes me to his cot.

My heart swells. 'It feels as if he has grown,' I whisper, and, picking up his warm, fat body, hold him close to mine. I breathe in the familiar scent of him and his newly shampooed hair. I don't know what I thought when Blake said his mother was in Thailand, but a cold hand had come into my body and clutched at my belly. I squeeze him harder against me. But now that he is in my arms again it is clear that my worries were unfounded.

'I usually just prick him with a pin when I want to wake him up,' Billie says.

I laugh, and the last remaining shadow of tension slips away. Sorab does not wake up and after a while I put him back into the cot.

Billie and I are chatting when Blake comes to the door. He greets Billie quickly and perfunctorily, his mind obviously preoccupied with other matters. He turns towards me—his mother wants us to meet her downstairs in the coffee lounge in an hour. Then he looks at Billie. 'Brian will knock on your door in an hour. Will you bring Sorab down then?' he asks with a frown.

'Sure.'

'Thanks, Billie,' Blake says.

'No problems.'

He takes my hand and turns to go, and then turns back. 'You did well to stand up to my mother.'

Billie flushes deep red with the compliment.

I only have time for a quick shower and a change of clothes before it is time to go downstairs. Unsure how I should dress and not really mentally prepared to meet my mother-in-law, I nervously slip on a shift dress over my bikini. I am on holiday after all, and it would be silly to get all dressed up.

Blake leans in and tells me I look a million dollars, but I am unable to stop the feverish and horrid sensation that I have been summoned to the headmistress's room.

As we enter the lounge I spot her instantly—blonde, blue-eyed, pale, and so carefully preserved she seems an ageless mannequin. There is not a single wrinkle on her face. Why, she could have been Blake's sister!

She is dressed in a dusky pink jacket that reminds me of the tooth powder that used to sit in my grandmother's bathroom cabinet. The most distinctive part of her appearance is the large piece of jewelry around her throat. It looks like the horned head of a bull. I have never seen anything like it. It is strange but beautiful, too. She does not rise as we approach.

As we near her Blake lets go of my hand, and goes around the low table to kiss her on both her cheeks. She lifts her chin and angles her head delicately to receive his kisses.

'Hello, dear,' she says quietly.

Blake straightens and regards her with an expression I cannot decipher. It is a mixture between exasperation and resignation.

'Why are you here, mother?'

'If Mohammed won't go to the mountain,' she murmurs.

Blake comes around and, putting his arm around my waist, says, 'Lana, meet my mother, Helena.'

'Hello, Lana.' Her voice is cool and slightly aloof, but not unfriendly. Her tone says 'approach, but come with caution'.

'Hello, Mrs. Barrington,' I say, overawed by her considerable presence.

'Helena,' she corrects with a nearly friendly smile.

'Helena,' I agree softly.

Blake gestures towards the sofa and I sink into it. He lowers himself beside me. She seems to be drinking still mineral water. A glass is half full with clear liquid and a bottle of it is on the table.

'Will you have something to drink?' she offers.

'Feel like some coffee?' Blake directs his question to me.

'Something cold.' My throat feels dry and scratchy.

A uniformed, smiling waiter stands beside Blake with a menu. Blake passes it to me and orders himself a short espresso.

I take the menu and feel Helena's eyes on me. I don't try to meet her eyes. Instead, I open the menu and bury myself in it. I look up at the waiter and order watermelon juice. The waiter moves away with a bow.

'Well,' Helena says.

'Whoever heard of a mother who interrupts her son's honeymoon?'

'Whoever heard of a son who doesn't invite his own mother to his wedding?'

'We saved some cake for you.' His voice is even, without provocation.

'I don't eat cake.'

Blake sighs. 'I'm sorry I didn't invite you, but I didn't want any trouble.'

'From what I heard, you had plenty anyway,' she retorts.

'Don't start,' Blake warns her.

'Well, it's the talk of the town. My best friends can't wait to call me up and tell me the big gossip.' She affects a hurt tone.

I bite my lip. Neither of them even seem aware of my presence. Really, Blake should have met her without me.

'Is that what you came all the way here to discuss?' Blake asks, the first sign of impatience edging his voice.

'No, as a matter of fact I came to see my grandson.'

'I can go get him,' I volunteer quickly.

Blake looks like he is about to protest.

But Helena turns to me with a smile. 'That'll be wonderful. Thank you, Lana.'

Smiling broadly I start edging away from them and sidling out from behind the table. In my haste I hit my knee on the edge of the table, and just about stop myself from crying out.

'Are you all right?' Blake asks, concerned.

I bob my head brightly and escape. When I get to the entrance I can't help it. I glance back quickly. Blake is watching me and his mother is watching him. I slip out quickly and meet Billie coming out of the lift. Brian is behind her. Brian nods unobtrusively at me and waits a few feet away.

Sorab squeals with unconcealed delight and excitement when he spots me. He holds his arms out and waves them impatiently at me. I take him from her and rain kisses on his face. He hugs my neck tightly and laughs.

'You look pale. You must have met the mutton dressed in dragon, then,' Billie says.

'Disconcertingly posh, isn't she?' I whisper.

'Yes, vomit-inducingly grand. What's it like so far?'

'*Alien vs. Predator.*'

She laughs. 'Which one's your husband?'

'Who wins?'

'Predator, I think.'

'That'll be him, then.'

'Don't let her bite you, duckie.'

'I won't.'

'Right, then, I'm off to do some sunbathing by the pool. Come and see me when you are finished,' she says and leaves, her flip-flops slapping the gleaming granite floor.

'See you later,' I call out after her, and, gazing adoringly at Sorab, drop more kisses on his face. He grins widely at me. 'So you missed your mummy, then?' I ask, and as if he has understood me, he grabs my neck and plants a very wet kiss on my lips.

'OK, let's go see your grandma.'

When we reach the door of the lounge I see that Blake and his mother are involved in an intense discussion. As soon as her eyes catch our arrival she stops talking, and, smiling widely, stands to greet her grandson.

'Oh, what a beautiful child,' she exclaims. 'Blue eyes and a round face. A moon child. Just like you, Blake,' she says.

'No, he's not,' Blake retorts harshly and I wonder what they are really referring to.

She laughs and holds her beautifully preserved hands, the tips pale pink ovals, out to Sorab.

But Sorab only buries his face in my neck, and looks longingly at his father, at the place where he really wants to go.

'He's a bit reserved with strangers,' I explain apologetically.

'Hello,' she coos brightly, but still buried in my hair, Sorab turns his face fractionally towards her, and stares at her unsmiling.

'He doesn't tend to say much,' I add.

Helena laughs. 'He's exactly like you, Blake. This is exactly how you were.'

I look at Blake. He is watching us without expression. When he catches my eyes, his lips curve upwards. Helena goes back to her seat and snaps open her white crocodile handbag with an expensive clunk, the discreet whiff of perfumed new leather, and a glimpse of the exclusive Gadino label. She fidgets about inside it and comes up with a lollipop, which she then unwraps slowly and deliberately, as she comes toward us. It is on the tip of my tongue to tell her that we have not introduced him to sweets or sugar, but I resist the urge. Fascinated, Sorab looks at the tantalizingly red lollipop. He wants it.

'Go on,' she encourages. 'It's for you.'

He snatches his hand out, but she pulls the sweet out of his reach. He stops and regards her. She opens her arms out and he rears back and watches her steadily. She offers him the lollipop and again he reaches for it only to have it drawn back. Any other child would have cried but he waits quietly, aware that it will be offered again. When it is, he lunges for it so hard, he almost jumps out of my arms. Helena is so taken aback by surprise that she doesn't react in time, and Sorab grabs the prize in his fat hands and falls back against me.

Before anyone else can take it away from him he pops it greedily into his mouth while eying Helena with a mixture of suspicion and curiosity. Helena laughs delightedly and turns toward Blake.

'Turns out he's a chip off the old block. He'll take, but he won't give.'

I gasp at the insult, but Blake stands and says smoothly, 'We have to go. I'm taking this little fellow here to the kiddie pool. Do you want to spend some time with him tomorrow morning?'

Helena smiles and nods gratefully, and for the first time I realize that she must have the normal instincts of a grandmother. At that moment my heart melts a little. She cannot be all bad. I will be as nice as I can to her.

'All right,' Blake says. 'I'll have the nanny come around to your suite at about eleven a.m., but please don't give him any more sweets.' Blake holds his hands out and Sorab eagerly leaves me for the higher perch.

Helena turns toward me. 'Will you have tea with me tomorrow, Lana?'

That takes me by surprise. I turn to look at Blake, but he is watching me expressionlessly. Up to me.

My hands are suddenly clammy. 'That will be nice,' I accept.

'Good, that's settled then. See you at four.'

'See you then,' I say, and we leave her at the table. I dare not glance back, but I can feel her eyes on us until we get out of the door, and turn the corner.

'Wow!' I say. 'That was intense.'

'You don't have to go tomorrow, you know?'

'I know that. I'll be OK,' I say, and kissing them both, go off in search of Billie.

I find Billie lying on her front on a sun lounger. Her bikini top is undone and her back is evenly brown. She opens her eyes and looks at me while I take off my shift dress and, rubbing some of the suntan lotion that her mother makes at home on my shoulders and stomach, sit down beside her.

'Well, did he bite her?' she asks languidly.

I slather more onto my arms. 'No, he didn't, but he tricked her into giving up her lollipop, and then refused to go to her afterwards.'

'Lollipop?' Billie says, lifting her head, suddenly cheered by the thought of a fresh grievance. 'That's not fair. How come I'm not allowed to give him sweets and she is?'

I smile inwardly and start on my legs. 'She's not either. Blake's already told her not to.'

She leans the side of her head on her elbow. 'What was his reaction to the lollipop?'

'His eyes nearly rolled to the back of his head, he liked it that much.'

She laughs. 'I hope you caught it on your phone?'

'No, I was too much in a state.' I put the lotion on the floor between us and lie down.

'Shame. I'd have loved to have seen it.'

I close my eyes. 'You know what? I'll keep Sorab tonight. You hit the town with Brian and enjoy yourself.'

'Are you sure?'

'Absolutely. I've really, really missed that mischievous, little runt. I've decided I'll never be so far away and so out of touch from him again. Besides, it's your holiday too.'

'OK,' she says. 'I'll go see one of those shows where the girls shoot ping-pong balls out of their fannies.'

I open my eyes. 'You're going to see a sex show?'

'Yeah, Brian's promised to take me.'

I laugh and lie back down. 'Right. Tell me all about it tomorrow at breakfast.'

'Do you want to have dinner at the Moon rooftop bar terrace?' Blake asks when I get back to the room.

'I know it's a must do, and I do, but not tonight. Tonight, can we just order room service and stay with Sorab?'

And so that is what we do. We have a beautiful night together, the three of us. After dinner, we bathe Sorab together, and play with him, until he gets tired. Then we take him to our bed and cuddle up together. Finally, as he does whenever Blake is around, he crawls on top of his father's body, and falls asleep.

We talk in whispers late into the night and go to sleep with Sorab's warm, small body tucked between us. My last thought as I fall into sleep is that I can't believe just how lucky I am.

# Seven
## Victoria Jane Montgomery

A nurse takes me to the evaluating psychiatrist later in the afternoon. The door opens and I see a man sitting at a desk. He is very still, but his eyes, behind his spectacles, are alert and intelligent. I can tell instantly that he is a man of great cultivation and charm who will speak with imagination and humor.

He stands and welcomes me as if I wasn't a patient, but a guest. It is an act, naturally, but one he excels at. You see, he wants to see me as whole, but he cannot help turning me into parts—the parts that work and those that don't.

I already know his name. One of the orderlies mentioned it and it is on his door. Dr. J. McBride. Anyway, he extends his hand, which surprises me. I put my hand in his and he looks at me with deliberately expressionless eyes. So he is hiding. He doesn't want me to know how very curious he is about the Montgomery heir who has fallen under his care.

I smile serenely at him.

Someone opens the door and calls him outside. I am not sure that it is not just a ruse to see what I will do left to my own devices. When he leaves I move toward the window. The vast grounds are empty. Patients are not allowed out. Smokers have a small barred balcony to do their deed. I gaze at the sky.

'What are you doing?' he says, from the door.

I turn to face him. 'Listening to the birdsong,' I lie. I had been thinking of the phoenix. Remembering that night when the sky had split open and he had dropped out of the light-filled crack. Wondering where he came from, where he has gone to.

He relaxes, his disquiet stilled. He is probably of the opinion that people who listen out for birdsong, whatever their inner difficulties, or however shattered, must be lovely, or harmless at worst.

'You were listening rather than watching,' he adds.

'Yes, yes. Exactly that. The starlings were Mozart's muse. Ein Musikalischer Spass.'

He smiles, pleased. It is now obvious to both of us that there could be something not quite right with me, but that I am definitely not mad.

'Birdsong is organized chaos,' he says.

I whip my head around. Ah, *Ordo ab chaos*. Order out of chaos. So: he is one of us. My father has seen to it. Excellent. Eventually it will be useful. I used to be too impatient to be a good chess player, but now I have the time. To think. To plan. To make my moves.

'Will you permit me to examine you?' he asks so graciously, it is as if I had a say in the matter.

I smile my acquiescence. It seems Dr. McBride and I will get on just fine.

The routine of a neurological exam is soothing: reflexes, muscle strength, coordination, tone, visual acuity, hearing, senses, and solving puzzles. Some are repeats I have already performed with the nurses, but I accept the intrusion demurely. When he scratches a pen on the soles of my feet I giggle and he looks at me with an expression that is almost one of fatherly concern.

'Tickles,' I explain, with a smile. He smiles back.

'That ought to do it,' he declares finally.

'I was wondering,' I begin casually, 'what are your thoughts on the subject of hallucinations?'

It is immediately obvious that it was a mistake to ask. A thin veil comes over his eyes.

'In the West there is cruel misunderstanding of the condition, often thought to portent madness so many people are unwilling to share their experiences. But in other cultures hallucinations are regarded as a privileged state of consciousness that is actively sought using hallucinogens, solitude, spiritual practices and meditation. Do you...have hallucinations?' His words are deeply enlightened but his eyes are a trap for the unwary. They watch me suspiciously.

'Just once, as a teenager, when I dropped an acid tablet,' I say softly.

 50

'Ah,' his voice clears. 'Do you ever hear voices or see things?'

I look at him calmly. 'No.'

The veil lifts. How easily I made that small doubt go away. 'At some stage we'll have to talk about what you did at the wedding, if that's all right?'

I smile tightly. 'Of course.'

'We'll need to examine that *particularly heightened state of anxiety* that you found yourself in.'

'I'm afraid I lost touch with reality. I was awfully depressed and angry. I didn't think. I've never done anything like that before. Besides, I wasn't really planning to hurt her. I just wanted to frighten her.'

He gazes at me, harmless as an old goat, as he tries to figure out if I am being honest.

I bend my head. 'Honest, I didn't mean to hurt her. And I am terribly sorry for what I did.'

And, surprisingly, he pats my hand reassuringly.

# Eight
## Lana Barrington

In the morning we go downstairs to an amazing buffet breakfast spread. The profusion of food is quite frankly a shock to me. A vast selection of local dishes, omelets made to order, rice porridge, toasts, cakes, pastries, cut fruit, different kinds of cereal. Blake has bacon and eggs and I have pancakes with maple syrup and fruit. Sorab nibbles on fruit.

Blake offers to keep Sorab for the day while I do some shopping with Billie. 'I want you to buy a very short, white dress. One of those stretchy materials if possible.'

'Why?'

'You'll find out tonight.'

'OK,' I agree with a grin. 'What will you guys do?'

'We haven't decided. It's between going to see the tigers or Kidzania.'

'Don't go see the tigers without me,' I wail.

'That's decided that, then. It will be Kidzania for us.'

'Thank you,' I say and plant a very noisy kiss on Sorab's nose, which he immediately wipes.

We leave the breakfast lounge together and separate in the lift. Sorab blows flying kisses as the lift doors close on us. I walk along the corridor and knock on Billie's door. She opens it with half-closed eyes, and walking away from me tumbles back into her bed.

'Good morning,' I say brightly.

'What time is it?' she croaks from under the pillow.

'After ten.'

She rolls off the bed and drags herself into the bathroom. I open the curtains to let the sunlight through the ceiling to floor windows. I am standing at the window looking out at Bangkok when she comes out in the hotel-provided robe, her face washed, and her wet hair wrapped in a towel.

'Have you had breakfast?' she asks.

'Yup. They have a beautiful spread downstairs. Want to go?'

'Are you kidding? I'm not eating that shite.'

She picks up the phone and orders breakfast: a bowl of jam and a glass of pineapple juice. I shake my head, and she raises one weary, don't-say-it eyebrow. She puts down the phone and goes to sit on the bed.

'So tell me about last night, then,' I urge impatiently.

Billie lights a fag, takes a huge lungful, and exhales slowly. 'Brian took me to Bangla Street. I was doing cartwheels with the excitement of seeing a live pussy show, and boy was that street crammed with touts selling ping-pong shows. They were so aggressive as well. One would grab your arm, you'd shake him off, and literally two feet later your arm would be grabbed again. They all carried like a large laminated menu of things the girls in their clubs could do with their pussies. Most of them acted too vague and shady when Brian asked about prices, saying that would be decided at the club. Anyway, one guy was willing to give Brian definite prices so we followed him.'

There is a knock on the door and Billie goes to open it. A hotel staff comes in with a tray of Billie's bowl of jam, a teaspoon and a glass of juice. She signs his receipt, tips him, and he goes out, closing the door after himself. Billie has a sip of her juice and lifts the dome to expose her bowl of jam.

'God, I'm starving,' she says. She grinds out her cigarette and, yanking the towel over her head, drops it on a chair. Lifting the spoon she starts spooning jam into her mouth as she walks to the bed. It never ceases to amaze me, no matter how many times I see it—Billie polishing off a bowl of jam for breakfast. I never thought a human being could exist on jam, chocolates, and pizza.

'There were about twenty-five different things the girls at his club could do. They could shoot ping-pong balls out of their fannies, sew with them, work their muscles so violently that they turned water into soda, open the tops of beer bottles.'

'Open a beer bottle?' I interject, shocked, despite myself.

She nods sagely. 'I wouldn't have believed it had I not seen it with my own eyes. The guy took us to this place—small and smoky, and lit up like a comedy club, but somehow very seedy. There were tables around a stage. We were given one that was so close I could rest my feet at the wooden edge of the stage. The only other people were an elderly European couple, a lone man with a huge beer belly—German probably—and a Chinese or Japanese couple huddled together looking bewildered.

'Anyway, we ordered our drinks. Apparently, what was unfolding on the stage was the last segment of another show. This girl was filling her vagina with ping-pong balls. She then shot them out with mind-zapping force at the audience. The funny thing was the elderly couple took a few in the chest and head and did not even flinch or duck as the balls hit them. No one clapped when it was over. It was all very odd.'

Billie scrapes her spoon on the bowl, licks the spoon and waves it around.

'She had straight, long hair, a cute little arse and a tattoo around her belly button which I really liked, but believe me, the only thing she communicated was boredom. I actually can't remember when I have seen someone look more bored. At this point a group of noisy Aussie surfer

boy types walked in. As they took their places a man brought a birthday cake and deposited it on the stage. The girl sat behind it, inserted a straw into her fanny, and blew out the six candles on it while the Aussie boys cheered her on with wolf whistles.'

Billie pulls a cigarette out of a box, lights it, and takes a full drag.

'Then she walked off and another girl walked on. This one, who looked pretty similar to the last one, danced and gyrated a few seconds around a metal pole and then came to the front of the stage, suddenly opened her legs, and fuck me, out plopped a live gerbil. The Aussies were loving it— they screamed and howled—but I was totally horrified.'

She shudders with the memory. 'You know how much I love gerbils. That's mental cruelty right there. The poor thing looked drenched and confused. It tried to run off, but the man who had brought the birthday cake came out from behind the curtains, picked it off by its tail, and walked off with it. That put me right off.'

From the time she told me about the gerbil my hand had flown to my mouth in shock. An uncomfortable giggle escapes me. 'What happened then?'

'Then she played a recorder with her pussy, which I have to admit was pretty damn impressive. And after that the way she then opened the beer bottle was fucking freaky. She simply squatted down over it, and popped its top off in seconds. By the time she turned water into soda water, the Aussies were starting to get downright rowdy, the single man was leaning forward eagerly, and I had started to feel icky about my moronic decision to go there. I felt really sorry for those women.'

She taps the ash off the end of her cigarette and scratches her leg where a mosquito had bitten her the night before.

'It's worse than being a prostitute. At least prostitutes suffer their degradations in private. But these poor women... All of them had the same blank expression. I guess mentally each one had switched off, and taken her mind to a different place.

'At that point I shot a look at Brian and he had an expression of pity on his face. So we left. But not before we had a massive row about the bill with a big woman on ugly pills and her walrus-faced helper. They had added all these extras on and inflated the bill by about ten times. Brian refused to pay and told them to call the police. That stopped them cold.'

I stare at Billie, not knowing what to say.

'I thought it was going to be fun and cool, but no one I saw was doing it for fun. Now I'm just sorry I ever went. I can't un-see it, and I feel like I've stolen a part of their pitiful souls. In the taxi later, Brian told me most of them are trafficked women who don't get paid hardly anything, and some have been seriously hurt while performing.'

'I guess we never realize how privileged and lucky we are until we see what some people's lives are like.'

'I just imagined it to be like some sort of circus, but it wasn't.'

I go up to her and take her hand. 'I'm sorry you feel bad, Billie, but I'm glad you didn't enjoy it. Every day we learn something about the world and about ourselves.'

'Oh, now might be the perfect time to tell you that I'm giving up the baby clothes business,' she announces.

'Why?' I ask, surprised.

She lifts one shoulder in a shrug.

'I thought you loved designing. And you are so awesome at it.'

She sighs. 'Well, I spoke to that accountant Blake sent me to, and it all boils down to two strategies. A: I make the clothes in England and sell them as exclusive designer gear in rich people's shops, or B: I reduce the quality so they can be mass produced by slaves in some third world country and flog them to ordinary people. Both options are almost equally repulsive to me.'

'So what do you want to do, then?'

'I want to work with your charity. Does it pay?'

'Yes, it pays,' I shriek happily. 'And I'd love to have you working with me.'

'Great. When do I start?'

I can't stop grinning. 'As soon as we get back. I'm still waiting for all the legal leg work and jargon to be over and done with, but the first thing

we are doing is supplying clean, free water in poor countries.'

'Clean, free water. Do *we* get that?'

I hesitate. 'Well, no.'

'So...'

'Billie, are you going to start? Or are we going to help these kids who have to walk for hours to fetch a pail of diseased water from the river?'

'Now that you put it like that.'

I shake my head at her. 'Sometimes...'

'Now might also be a good time to tell you that I'm having my boobs done.'

'What?' I exclaim, surprised by the sudden change in topic, and the topic itself. 'The shocks are coming in thick and fast today.'

She smiles wickedly. 'I've always wanted big, beautiful breasts. And yesterday I realized that if I can't be small and delicate like these Thai girls, then I want horribly perfect, overtly sexual melons on my chest. I think I'd like the idea of socking a man for looking at my cleavage, and not my eyes, while he is talking to me.'

'You're one strange girl, Billie.'

She puts the empty bowl and spoon on the tray, lights another cigarette, and inhales languidly. 'I know,' she sighs dreamily.

We spend what's left of the morning shopping at Siam Paragon. I manage to find a short white Lycra dress as per Blake's instructions.

'Very racy,' is Billie's comment.

Billie buys herself a pair of gold hotpants she saw one of the hookers wearing the night before and a sequined Sandringham blue tank top.

'Don't worry. They're not to be worn together,' she assures me.

After lunch we return to the hotel and we agree to meet by the pool in half an hour, but after a few laps in the afternoon heat I am already exhausted. Billie takes the nanny and Sorab back with her, and Blake and I go back to our suite. Blake gets on with some work while I go up the flight of black wooden stairs and get into the shower.

It is nearly three when I come out. I can hear Blake downstairs on the telephone. I switch on the hairdryer. The water or the heat has made it a little flyaway so I end up clipping the sides with two brown slides. I apply some lip gloss and some mascara and then I stand in front of the six dresses I have brought with me indecisively.

I try them all on, discard all six, and then go back to the first one, which is a short-sleeved, rather bold affair with large, bright flowers. It slips over my head like liquid. I smooth it down my hips and look at myself critically. Perhaps the plain blue dress will be a better choice. I look at the blue dress. Maybe it is a tad too short. I flash a smile at my reflection. And then a scowl. Oh, what the hell! I'll just wear this.

I take the slides off and tie my hair back with a red ribbon and add a shimmer of fragrance. When I come down the stairs, Blake is sitting at the dining table working. He looks up from his work and whistles, which is a good thing, because if he approves then Helena probably will, too.

He puts his elbows on the table, next to his green coconut drink, and smiles an angelic smile. The sun is coming in through the large glass wall behind him and he looks positively edible. 'Come here,' he mouths.

Oh man, this man could charm birds out of a tree. 'No way,' I mouth back.

'Are you seriously disobeying me, Mrs. Barrington?'

I nod.

A dark chuckle rips through him. He raises his eyebrows. 'Are you sure about this?' he asks.

I glance at the door. It is no more than ten feet away, and he is at least thirty away. And he is seated. I can definitely make it. Grinning cheekily at him I make a dash for the door.

I run like every horned devil in hell is after me. I am breathing hard and laughing as I grasp the doorknob. An iron-strong embrace crushes me, still laughing and breathless, into a big male chest. My eyes travel upwards and collide with his. His are magnificent, dancing with laughter and mischief. Nice mischief. And a wicked, wicked sliver of desire. His scent is like a sweet mist around me. Hot fingers tease my nape. Other fingers are at my skirt, dragging it upwards.

'Don't you dare,' I warn breathlessly, but my voice is fluttery, lacks any real conviction.

'No woman should go and see her mother-in-law without a little lick.'

I groan, 'No,' and try to wriggle out of his hold.

'Or yes, that feels good.'

I stop wriggling. 'This is a bad idea. You're going to muss up my clothes,' I scold, even though, like a starved little thing, my sex is already yearning for his tongue.

He laughs, the sound deep and coconut-scented. 'It's the best idea I've had all year. No one will ever know,' he purrs silkily.

My skirt climbs steadily. Fuck it. He is going to have his way. I know it. I can taste it. I can sense it searing in his blood... And mine.

'I can't let poor pussy go to a chilly hotel suite with the air conditioning turned up too high. Poor thing, all alone, and barely covered.'

I crack a smile and lean back against the door. 'Good job, Barrington, dragging me kicking and screaming to exactly where I want to go.'

The wandering hand arrives at my inner thigh. His palm is warm on my bare skin. Suddenly he is no longer over and above me, but underneath my skirt. I throw my head back and laugh. I'm not going to be laughing for long. Fingers creep under the gusset of my knickers and pull it to one side. Other fingers part me open. A warm mouth latches onto my cleft, and sucks me out as if I am an oyster, raw and about to lose its insides.

Oh, yeah.

See? Told you I wouldn't be laughing for long.

Radiant heat glows between my legs. I close my eyes and allow the never-stopping, never-easing shimmering magic to work. He doesn't mess about and I crest quickly.

He licks up the juices, replaces the material over my slit, and comes up, lips wet and smiling. Wonderfully warm and glowing, I stretch languorously and smile up at him mistily.

'Now that's how a girl should be sent to see her mother-in-law.'

'Blake?'

'What?'

'What if she doesn't like me?'

He shrugs nonchalantly. 'And so what? You're not married to her.'

'She's not going to like me, is she?'

'Why do you need her to like you?'

'I don't know. I just thought it might be nice. Nobody wants their mother-in-law to hate them.'

'Well, my darling, just remember what I told you. The less you try to placate her, the more chances you have of being "liked" by her.'

'Do you think this dress makes me look like a municipal flower bed?'

He smiles. 'You look like a prize-winning mixed seed packet blooming in summer.'

'Is that a compliment?'

'You bet it is,' he says and opening the door gently pushes me into the corridor.

# Nine

I ring the bell of her suite and a woman in a mannish suit and a brisk efficient air opens the door. She invites me into the suite with a professional smile and introduces herself as Ann Rivers, Helena's personal assistant. The air conditioning has been turned up so high I shiver slightly. She leads me into the dining room. A Thai waitress waiting by the sideboard bows from the neck and puts her palms together as if in prayer.

I return the gesture and look around me to a table that has been set to the nines. There are all kinds of cutlery and all kinds of food that I don't recognize. There is also a sideboard full of dishes in covered stainless steel warmers. I bite my lip with consternation.

Of all the settings Helena could have picked, this I consider the most intimidating. As I am standing there she walks in from the opposite doorway. She has timed it brilliantly and I look at her with some awe. There is something very commanding about this beautiful woman. She has what my mother called star quality. As soon as she walks into a room she dominates it utterly, the way a full moon dominates the entire night sky.

She is wearing a classic tan and black hounds tooth suit over a black turtleneck sweater, and her hair and face are immaculate. Her choice of a turtleneck sweater in this climate surprises me a bit. She smiles at me. The smile carries genuine warmth in it, and I smile back. Maybe this will turn out all right. Ann retreats unobtrusively.

'Do have a seat,' she invites and points to a chair at one end of the table. The table is large enough to seat six. Helena then takes her place at the head of the table.

The Thai waitress pushes the chair in as I sit down, and whipping a napkin open, lays it expertly across my lap.

As the waitress does the same with Helena I look nervously at the utensils around me. Why on earth did I imagine that this was meant to be a casual tea, some finger sandwiches, warm scones and a few slices of cake?

'Well, this is nice,' I say. My voice sounds higher than normal.

'Yes, quite. I thought we should get to know one another,' Helena tells me. Her voice is soft and friendly, far more so than yesterday. 'I want to know all about you and how you met Blake.'

Oh no, you don't, I think, but I smile politely. 'We met through a mutual acquaintance.'

'Ah, of course. Who was it?'

'Rupert Lothian.'

She tries to frown, but the Botox stands in the way. 'Never heard of him. Who is he?'

'I...er...worked for him.'

She looks at me. 'That's nice.' There is an expression in her eyes that makes me suspect she knows exactly who Rupert is, and exactly how I met Blake.

She picks up a small white jar that is near her right hand. I notice that I, too, have a similar jar to my right hand. Mine contains milk. I watch her pour the milk in her jar into what I had assumed was a fingerbowl. She fills it to one-third and looks at me. Her expression is almost quizzical. She smiles, as if she can't understand why I am not doing the same.

I smile back, and, quickly lifting my jar, copy her. I cannot imagine how the milk will be used. Perhaps we will be dipping something into it.

When I look at her again, she is still smiling, but her smile is cold and hard. You are not one of us, no matter what you do, wear, et cetera—we will sniff you out, her eyes tell me. She bends and puts the bowl of milk on the floor. Straightening and meeting my eyes, hers shining with malice, she calls out, 'Constable, here, boy. Milk.'

Fiery heat rushes up my neck and cheeks. For a second, I am frozen with horror at the vindictiveness with which she has deliberately tricked me. Blake was right. I should never have tried to be accepted by her. And then I straighten my shoulders and smile, the kind of smile I never thought I would be able to accomplish. Coldly.

Their kind of smile. Something changes in her eyes. How quick she is to recognize a worthy opponent.

Constable, a small, white handbag dog, is noisily lapping up the milk. For a little while there is only the sound it makes and the low hum of the air conditioning.

Then, I reach for a tiny morsel of food. It is round and blue. I do not recognize it, and I do not care. I pick it up with my fingers and daintily pop it into my mouth. Beyond the first impression of it being warm and soft with some sweet filling, I do not register anything else. Chewing steadily, I meet Helena's eyes, and hers are surprised and slightly horrified by my uncouth manners. Oh, but, I'm not finished yet, Helena. I turn to the woman in the starched outfit standing by the sideboard.

'Oh, hello,' I say cheerfully. 'What's your name?'

Her dark, almond eyes widen with surprise, perhaps even alarm. No doubt they teach her what they used to tell the African American slaves— A room with you in it must seem empty.

'My name is Somchai,' she says, bowing her head deferentially. Her voice is barely a whisper.

'Come and try this, Somchai. I'd like you to taste it and tell me what is in it,' I invite expansively.

She looks confused and shoots a worried glance at Helena.

'Oh! Don't worry about Helena. She won't mind,' I dismiss airily. 'I'm sure she wants to know what she is eating too.'

Somchai comes forward timidly. 'I don't need to taste. I can tell you what all the different dishes are.'

'Oh, that will be nice. Do, please.'

'What you have just eaten is a coconut hotcake. It is like a mini pancake with different sweet fillings.' She points to the dish not with her forefinger but with her hand made into a small fist and the thumb jutting out to form a polite pointer. 'And this one here is fried shrimp with glutinous rice. This one is taro root mixed with flour and turned into balls. That over there is called golden threads. They are strings of egg yolk quickly, quickly boiled in sugar syrup. Next to it is grass jelly. That one there is money bags: crispy, deep fried pastry purses filled with minced pork, dried shrimp and corn wrapped in cha phlu leaves.'

I nod as if I am fascinated by her descriptions while she works her way down the table and starts on the covered dishes warming on the sideboard. Rice field crab cakes served with green papaya salad, salt beef dumplings, fermented pork neck sausages with ginger, tiny banana leaf cups filled with ant and chicken eggs, grilled cuttlefish stuffed inside jackfruit, and yuck... Fried silk worm pupae.

'Wow! What a feast,' I cry, my voice unnaturally shrill and bright. 'There is too much here for two. Would you like to join us, Somchai?' Without giving her the chance to answer, I instruct genially. 'Come on. Pull up a chair beside me.'

Helena gasps, which gladdens my heart no end, but poor Somchai suddenly looks terrified. A small animal getting crushed in the middle of two fighting elephants.

She shakes her head slightly. 'Thank you very much. It is too kind of you, but I have already eaten.'

I take pity on her. 'Oh, that's a shame. Never mind then. Maybe next time.'

Somchai shoots another nervous glance at Helena.

And Helena takes that opportunity to take control of the situation. 'That will be all. You can go now,' she dismisses coldly.

I turn to look at her. Her mouth is a thin, disapproving line.

Somchai bows from the neck first in Helena's direction and then in mine. Then she scuttles away as quickly as she can, never to be seen again. As soon as the door closes, Helena looks at me.

'Are you quite finished?' she seethes quietly.

'As a matter of fact, yes,' I say, and sweep upward regally.

'Sit down, Lana,' Helena grates. 'You've made your point. There is no point in carrying on with this childishness.'

It occurs to me that she started it, but I obey. She is right. Some kind of truce needs to be declared.

'How do you have your tea?'

Now that Somchai has been dismissed, I realize that we are going to have to serve ourselves if we are going to eat and drink. I stand, and picking up the teapot, take it over to her. Carefully, I fill her tea cup while she steadfastly keeps her eyes on the tea pouring into her cup. I can smell her hairspray.

'Thank you,' she says, and I cease pouring.

'Sugar?'

She shakes her head.

'Milk?' I enquire innocently.

She looks up at me then, her eyes sharp, cunning as a crocodile. 'Thank you.'

I glance at the empty jug stationed beside her beringed hand and watch her hand spasm into a fist. Returning to my side, I fill my cup silently with tea and put two sugars into it. Then I return the milk from the bowl back into the jug, and taking it over to her and positioning the jug above her cup of tea begin pouring. She raises her hand to indicate when she has had enough. I take the jug back to my end of the table and sitting down pour some milk into my cup. Silently I stir my milk.

'I have an issue to take up with you.'

I raise an eyebrow.

'I'm not happy about that creature you have taking care of my grandson.'

My mouth hangs open with astonishment. I snap it shut, as mad as a cut snake. Now she has gone where she definitely shouldn't have. 'That creature happens to be my best friend, and I will thank you not to refer to her as such again in my presence.'

'That woman with a neck that looks like a public lavatory wall is your *best* friend?'

The arrogance and snobbery is breathtaking. I take a deep and cleansing breath before I dream of answering her. 'Has she done anything that makes you believe she is unfit to care for *your* grandson?'

Her eyes flicker insolently. She has done that on purpose to provoke me. The white, perfectly manicured fingers of her right hand are resting delicately on the table top. The air conditioning hums like a lazy insect. It is actually too cold in this room. I'm starting to get chicken skin on my arms and legs. I wonder if she has turned it up on purpose. No wonder she is wearing a turtleneck sweater.

I come to the conclusion that one of the things I detest and deeply resent most is being in a freezing hotel room with my mother-in-law.

'Well,' I say quietly, 'I'd rather be her than a bloodline snob, any day.'

She smiles cynically. 'Are you sure? You seem to have done everything in your power to…catch a bloodline snob in your net.'

'By some quirk of fate I find myself married to one, but I can assure you I wouldn't want to be one of you.'

'You don't seem to understand. Our bloodline can be traced back to antiquity, beyond recorded history. We, the thirteen original families, have been in power since time immemorial. We are born to lead. It is the design of the current paradigm. Our bloodline is a privilege. You cannot join the family. You must be born into it. There is no other way in. So you can *never* be one of us.'

She stops and takes a delicate sip of tea and I stare at the sheer hubris of the woman.

'And just so you are aware, breeding is case specific, depending on the role required. There are no 'unapproved' unions. Our families always intermarry between houses. In all my time on this earth I have never seen or heard of a family member breaking this code.'

'Your son just did.'

She carries on as if I had not spoken. 'In the rare instance of a child being born in…well…difficult circumstances, that child will be raised in accordance with the family rules, but away from either of its parents. To serve the family.'

My heart hammers in my chest. 'Is that what you have planned for Sorab?'

Her words chill me to the bone. 'Everybody serves the family. One way or another.'

'Well, Sorab is not. He is my son and I will die before I give him up to the "family".'

Swollen with vanity she sits at her fine table and smiles knowingly, but I know how to prick her. 'Did you know what your husband was doing to your son?'

She doesn't pretend not to understand. Her eyes flash with anger. 'You must be very proud of yourself. Rising up from the lowest rung of society, snaring a man such as *my son* and now presuming to sit in judgment of me. How old are you?'

'Twenty-one.'

'And you think you know how everything works, do you?'

How clever she is. Suddenly I am under attack again. 'I know fathers shouldn't abuse their sons,' I say.

She scowls and flushes with rage. 'Abuse? How dare you? Who said anything about abuse?'

For a moment I am so taken aback by her genuine anger that I start to think she did not know, and that I have accused her wrongly, and my brain instinctively scrambles to apologize, but her next words make me realize that she is not angry because I accused her, but because I have dared to question the ways of her precious bloodline.

Her voice is abruptly and disconcertingly quiet and mild. 'There is a tribe in Asia, untouched by Western influence,' she pauses to smile sarcastically. 'Something you, no doubt, will advocate preserving. The custom of this tribe is that when the husband comes home from a hard day's hunting, he puts down his hunting accouterments, and goes up the steps of his wooden house to call to his daughter—usually she will be very young, less than ten, perhaps even five or less. When he calls her, she knows what he wants of her and she will go to him and lie down, usually in the main room where everyone can see what is going on. He will open her small legs, and right there in front of his wife and all his other children, he will put his mouth between her legs and he will *suck*.'

She stops to savor my unconcealed horror. 'Often while he is drinking from her innocent little pussy, she will be drinking from her milk bottle.'

I stare at her in shock. Is she telling the truth?

'You don't believe me?' she challenges. 'Go look it up.' Her face morphs into a hard, cold mask. 'Mind you, only the father has this privilege. This act, no matter what it may seem like to your education and understanding, has no sexual connotation to it at all. It is done to strengthen the man. As the girl grows and becomes a woman, the practice is no longer considered strengthening and is discarded. But the girl will carry fond memories of the times she has 'helped' her father. After all, it must be a rather pleasant exchange.'

She pauses, and, picking up a pair of chopsticks, reaches for and expertly captures the dried shrimp and corn wrapped in cha phlu leaves. 'Will you be the intrepid woman who will go and inform this tribe that what they are doing is shameful and barbaric?'

I swallow hard, bereft of words.

'No? And yet you are happy to sit here and lecture me on the barbaric nature of *our* ways and our rituals.'

This woman is truly a master at mind games. Every time I think I have her cornered, I find that I am the one in the corner. 'If these girls remember their encounters as fond memories then how can they be compared to what happened to Blake? He still suffers from awful nightmares.'

'I am surprised at you. What kind of woman encourages her husband to be weak?'

A bark of laugher erupts from me. 'Weak?'

'Children have nightmares about their visits to the dentist. Would you have them not visit the dentist?'

I throw my hands in the air in exasperation. I feel as if I am caught in the twilight zone. This woman is totally nuts. I stand up. 'I'm going. Thanks for the tea.'

She remains seated. 'I am leaving tomorrow, but I will see you in Belgium for the July ball. It is our most important gathering. Blake will want to "introduce you", I'm sure.'

I look her in the eye. 'I won't be going.'

For the first time I see that I have confounded her. She did not expect that. It never crossed her mind that anyone would refuse such an important invitation. I take the milk jug and pour the milk back into the bowl. Then I place it on the ground.

'Here, Constable. Here, boy,' I call. The little dog jumps up from its prone position and runs toward the bowl. I straighten and she is watching me. Her mouth is a thin line, her jaw is tight.

'Goodbye, Helena. I don't think we'll ever meet again.'

'Don't think you can keep Blake from the gathering.'

'Blake is welcome to go. That will be his decision.'

'You're making a mistake, a big mistake.'

'I don't think so,' I say quietly, and leave her room. I take the lift and go back to our suite. I feel so odd, so small. At our suite Blake is waiting for me. He takes me into his arms.

'How did it go?'

'It went exactly as you thought it would.'

'I'm sorry. I know you wanted it to go well.'

'It was silly of me to think it would go any other way. I am the worst person you could have married, aren't I?'

He grins. 'It would have been worse if I had married Billie.'

That makes me giggle. 'Do you know she said Billie's neck looked like the wall of a public lavatory?'

One side of his lips lift, as his heart-stopping, long lashes sweep down. 'That's mother for you.'

'Joking aside, she really hates me, doesn't she?'

'She doesn't hate you. She is jealous of you. She'd give up all her money and privilege to be you.'

'Me?'

'Everything you take for granted, the apple-like tightness of your cheeks, the firmness of your body, the light in your eyes. They are a cause of great envy for those who have passed that stage.'

'How sad that we all have to grow old.'

He looks into my eyes. 'I've ordered you high tea.'

I frown. 'You have?'

'Hmm…' He takes me by the hand to the dining table. It is laid out with a proper English tea. Finger sandwiches, scones, cream, raspberry jam, cakes.

I look at him and feel like bursting into tears.

'You knew she'd do that.'

'I didn't know. I guessed. But I had to let you try.'

'Oh, my darling,' I ramble. 'I love you so much nobody even knows how much because that's just how much I love you.'

'OK,' he agrees with a wide grin.

# Ten
## Victoria Jane Montgomery

'Hello, Mummy,' I greet softly.

'Hello, dahhling,' she witters excitedly, and coming forward, grasps my shoulders and kisses both my cheeks soundly. Her blue eyes are crinkled at the corners, but deep within them I see something disconcerting. It is not I but she who is dancing on the edge of madness.

'How are you?' she asks, her voice still an untamed shriek.

My mother and I have never been close, but I can see now that she can be my most useful ally. I smile my sweetest smile at her. 'I feel fine.'

'I thought it was going to be a horrible day, but hasn't it turned out so lovely?'

Of course. The weather. She is talking about the weather as if I am a stranger that she has met at the village bakery. Very English. Sure. I can do that. I turn toward the window. The sun is shining. 'Yes, you are right, it is a beautiful morning.'

My mother's right hand floats uncertainly up toward her face and suddenly she seems a pitiful creature. 'Are they treating you well?'

'Yes, everyone is very nice.'

'Oh good.' She sighs, and appears relieved.

'How is Daddy?'

'Well, he misses you, of course. He can't wait for when you are better, when you will be allowed to return,' she says brightly.

'When do you think that will be, mother?'

Mother blinks uncertainly. She honestly reminds me of a deer caught in headlights. 'Well, as soon as you are better, my dear.'

Ah, no time soon then, but she is still speaking.

'Don't worry about that now. Just get better quickly. Take all your medicines and do everything the doctors tell you, can't you? You'll be home in the blink of an eye. Come and stay with us for a while. I've never liked the idea of you staying alone in that flat in London, anyway.'

'Yes, that's a good idea. I will.'

She smiles, pleased at the thought of me staying with them. 'Would you like me to bring you anything the next time I come?'

'Yes, as a matter of fact I'd like to read some of the books you read.'

Mummy frowns. 'But I only read romances.'

'Yes, they will do nicely.'

'But you hate them.'

'I've changed my mind. The library here is in quite a disgusting state. It almost entirely consists of the third part of trilogies.'

She smiles broadly. 'Yes, I'll bring you some of my favorite books.'

I look at her brooch. It is not her best one. 'Mummy, can I have that brooch you are wearing?'

Her hand flutters to it. 'This?'

I nod.

She frowns in consternation. She cannot understand why I might want her brooch. 'Why?'

'I'd just like to keep it while I am here. It'll remind me of you. At night. When it gets lonely.'

'Of course, of course.' She takes it off with trembling hands and brings it to me.

'Thank you, Mummy.' Our fingers touch and before she can remove her hand I catch the smooth, slightly knobby fingers. Her eyes run upward to meet mine—hers are startled and a little frightened. She is now afraid of me. Afraid of what I am capable of.

'I haven't been a very good daughter, have I?'

The little liar begins to shake her head, quite vehemently too.

'I know,' I continue, 'that I haven't been a good daughter. I've been too…obsessive.'

She draws a sharp breath. This is territory that she has been warned not to go into. We might end up talking about that terrible thing that I did to Blake's slut. She rushes. 'Don't worry about all that now. You just get better.'

'Thank you, Mummy. I was wondering if you could bring me some of my jewelry, too, perhaps the designer pieces. It will make me feel better while I sit here.'

'Of course, but what if the staff or the other patients pinch it?'

I shrug. 'Then you'll bring me some more. They are not too expensive to replace.'

She smiles, a ray of sunshine in her worried face. 'I'll bring a little safe for you.'

'Thank you, Mummy.'

She sighs.

'Do you know this might have been the best thing that's ever happened to me, after all?'

'Oh?'

'I was too spoilt and selfish. I think I'd like to build new bridges with you and Daddy. Start afresh and all that. I hope with time,' I pause and drop my head, 'you and Daddy and Blake...and his wife will find it in your hearts to forgive me for what I have done.'

'Oh, darling. There is nothing to forgive. Certainly not on my side, anyway.'

'I disgraced you and Daddy.'

'Never mind. No use crying over spilt milk.'

'I think the meds are helping. I feel a lot calmer now. A bit as if I am floating on a cloud.'

She smiles. 'Probably a good thing. You've always been a little intense.'

I laugh. And so does she. She will be my ally.

After a while she leaves. I am happy to see her go. I find her exhausting, but I need her. I stand at the window. I can see Daddy's Rolls parked close to the entrance. I wait by the window until I see her emerge from the building and cross the road. As she is about to get into the car, someone enters my room. I turn around.

It is Angel. I smile at her.

'How are we today?' she says. Her voice is jaunty.

'I have a surprise for you,' I say.

'When people say that to me it usually means they have soiled the bed or something equally revolting.'

I open my palm and show her the brooch.

She gasps and comes forward. 'Oh, it's beautiful, Lady Victoria.' And then she stops and looks at me. 'It's real, isn't it?'

'Of course.'

'I don't think we are allowed to take such expensive gifts from the patients.'

'I won't tell if you won't.'

'Well,' she says doubtfully.

'Besides, I'm not allowed jewelry. Let alone something so sharp.'

'That's true. It is very sharp. You could hurt yourself with it.'

'Exactly. Why don't we trade?'

'Trade?' Her tone becomes suspicious.

'In exchange, you let me use your cell phone sometimes to make local calls. How about that?'

'Local calls.'

'Just to friends and family, if I start to miss them too much...'

Her face changes. 'I guess that would be OK.'

'Oh thank you, Angel. You don't know how happy you've made me. Thank you.' I take a step forward and place the brooch into her palm.

We look at each other—both our eyes are shining. She doesn't know it, but both of us have just made a bargain with the devil.

# Eleven
## Lana Barrington

There is hardly a breeze to ameliorate the relentless humidity that extends into the night like the embrace of an unwanted lover. The wet heat hits us like a wall when we exit the hotel. We have dinner in a beautiful restaurant in the middle of Bangkok then Blake takes me to a club. It is darkly lit, smoky, and throbbing with sultry music, but it is also air conditioned and wonderfully cool. It seems full of European men and scantily clad, snake-hipped local girls. All the tables and booths face a round stage.

'What is this place?' I ask Blake.

'It's a place where everything is allowed.'

There is a stage lit with a red light.

We are taken to a booth by a girl in a lace bustier, leather knickers and black stockings. 'You like something to drink?' she asks.

'Give us a couple of your most potent cocktails,' Blake says.

She nods, smiles and leaves.

I look around me. 'We are in a sex club, aren't we?'

Blake grins. 'I love that it's taken you all this time to figure that out.'

The drinks arrive, umbrellas galore. I take a sip. It is deceptively cloying. I should be careful. I have already had a few over dinner.

'I've changed my mind. Get me a whiskey,' Blake tells the waitress.

She nods and leaves.

The blue neon light comes on over the stage. A girl walks on. She is dressed in a white bikini top and matching thong. The costume glows against her dusky skin. She has long black hair that reaches her waist. A tiny little man with a sickly yellow complexion runs in front of her and deposits a stool at the edge of the stage. She gyrates and dances around the stool. I have a sudden fear that she is going to drop a wet gerbil.

Slowly she peels her sticky thong off. Underneath she is wearing a Brazilian wax. I squirm in my seat. The memory of Billie telling me she felt as if she had stolen a part of their soul by watching them is still fresh in my mind. Besides, I am jealous, I am not sure I want Blake to be watching this. He turns his eyes toward me.

'Just think of her as a performer. I only want you.'

I look into his eyes. Unconvinced, I touch him between the legs. He is un-aroused. It may be childish of me, but that makes me feel a whole lot better. I leave his eyes and concentrate on the stage. The girl sits on the stool and suddenly lifts her legs athletically off the ground. With her knees held straight she opens them into a wide V towards the audience. All her bits are exposed to the audience. A spotlight is shone onto her vagina. It is an uncomfortable moment for me. I keep thinking that Blake might be attracted to her. I hate the thought.

I take a huge gulp of my drink. The same man who brought the stool brings a cigarette box to her! He offers it to her and she takes one. With a face as serious as murder he lights it for her and she puts it into her mouth. I stare with astonishment as she transfers the cigarette from her mouth to her vagina and starts blowing perfect smoke rings! I turn to Blake, but he is looking at me.

'I don't want to watch.'

'Then don't,' he murmurs in my ear. I feel his hand slide up my thigh.

'Blake,' I protest.

'Everything is allowed here. You didn't really think I came to see that performance, did you?'

'What did you come for?' I ask breathily.

'I came here to fuck in public.'

I draw in a mortified breath. 'What?'

I feel his fingers moving up my thighs, parting them and entering me.

'No,' I say, shaking my head, but the alcohol I have consumed at dinner is singing in my blood, and the blood is pounding in my veins. A crackle of magical static is throbbing wetly between my legs.

'Nobody can see us. And,' he adds persuasively, 'even if they can we will never see them again. So what do you care what they think?

The truth is I don't. I look around me, and indeed nobody is looking at us. It even seems as if there are other couples in various stages of the act.

'Take off your panties.'

I slip my fingers into my new stretchy white dress, hook them into my lacy bits and pull them down. Bending slightly I take them off and put them into his waiting hand. He pockets them. Turning slightly he faces me and opens my thighs.

My body is lust drenched and impatient for some hot action, but that is so direct I gasp and look around nervously. 'I'm not sure this is such a good idea.'

He ignores my comment and, lifting me up, puts me on his lap so my body is facing him, my thighs spread, my sex touching his erection. His hands pull my dress until it is bunched around my hips.

'Straight to the point then,' I rasp.

He puts his middle finger into his mouth and—I close my eyes because I know what he is going to do, and I am both embarrassed and excited by it—slowly inserts that saliva lubricated finger between my legs.

He smiles arrogantly. His hair glows blue-black in the blue tinted spotlights. Tonight he oozes danger and power…and something bad. I like it.

'You want me to do what?'

He chuckles. Even that sound seems illicit and dancing with power tonight. 'Show me that this is a mutual appreciation society.'

I unbutton the top button of his jeans and slide the zip down, to see the tip of his erection poking out of his underwear. 'Oh, you animal, you,' I tease. My thighs twitch as I release his shaft. It bounces out and I stop with a gasp. My eyes run into his, shocked, questioning.

'You're...different,' I say.

He laughs.

'What have you done?'

'An old woman came by while you were out shopping and expertly stung me with two bees.'

'What?'

'You heard.'

'When you say old, how old was she?'

'At least ninety-seven and she was only about four feet tall.'

I laugh breathlessly. 'Did it hurt?'

'Like two mosquito bites.'

I drop my scandalized eyes down to his exposed cock. It seems massively swollen, brutally aggressive, and...well, thrilling.

'Do you like it?' he purrs.

'I don't know, yet. I kind of liked it before too.'

His eyes glint. 'Try it and then complain.'

Right, when in Rome... 'That can be arranged,' I say huskily.

Holding the swollen shaft by the base I lower myself onto it and slide down its hard length slowly, conscious of the unfamiliar feeling of being

so incredibly stretched and filled. I get halfway and have to take a deep breath.

'You are soooo much bigger and thicker,' I whisper in his ear.

'It's creepy how obsessed I am with you,' he rumbles from deep within his chest, and taking my chin in his fingers pulls my lips to his. I gasp into his mouth, and fight for his tongue, bring it into my mouth, and suck it. Every nerve in my body feels alive, with his tongue in my mouth and my sex unbearably stretched. The kiss deepens. Breathlessly, I feel my dazzled body being slowly pushed down the thick shaft. He takes his mouth away from me and says something but I don't hear.

I am all sensation. The music, the smoky air, the sounds of other people having sex. He takes my nipples in his fingers and tugs them, but so gently, they ache for a good sucking in his mouth. All the while he is shoving his cock deeper and deeper into me. I moan helplessly as I squirm downwards. The breeze from an air con vent blows chilled air over our heads. Smoke curls around us like ghostly snakes or dragons. Anyone can see us and what we are up to but I don't care.

My tiny, entirely complete world of him, me and his bee-stung cock is rudely interrupted when I feel a hand on my shoulder. The touch is light but utterly alien and unwelcome. My hands grip Blake's shoulders as my head swivels back with the same creeped out horror as having a spider fall on my bare skin.

A woman is standing next to me. Like most of the other local girls in that club, she has straight, long black hair and is scantily clad in a bikini bra and shiny black shorts. Under the spotlights her skin glows smooth and moon pale.

'Can I join you?' she asks. Her accent is Americanized.

She is touching me and asking me, but she is looking at Blake. My mind goes blank except for the weird thought that Billie would probably like her small-boned girl-body. Me? I look at the bulletproof lipstick, almond eyes, and the totally impenetrable expression and I think—poison!

The shock and embarrassment of being caught sitting on a dick wears off dead quick and my mating response takes over, and it is so instinctive, so animalistic, and so loaded with the threat of actual violence that it shocks another detached, watching part of myself. *No, I fucking wouldn't like you to join in.* I actually want to hiss at her. If I had fangs I would have bared them at her.

The air crackles with my sudden animosity.

Blake's voice cuts into my simmering rage. 'No. You can't,' he tells her, his voice edged not with the fury I am experiencing, but simply with impatience at being interrupted.

She slinks away wordlessly and I watch her go, still in a jealous fury.

'I don't want to share you with her or anyone,' he whispers in my ear, and I am suddenly euphoric because damn, if I didn't loathe even more the thought that he might have wanted her to join in.

I turn back to look into his eyes. His gaze locks with mine, mesmeric, dizzying, sweetening the poisoned air. Making a protective cage around us. He is looking at me so hungrily, it is as if I am food or prey. I latch onto the hunger eagerly. This is my mate. And only mine.

'Baby,' he growls. His voice is so full of hot lust, its vibration sizzles through me, intoxicating me. I exhale, almost a moan. He gets harder and bigger inside.

I grip him with my thighs. Looking deep into my eyes he grabs my bare ass with his powerful hands, ramming me all the way down that pillar of meat. 'It's all for you,' he says with a dark laugh.

'Fuck, yeah,' I cry hoarsely. And I feel myself flush with the feeling, the indignity of total possession.

He begins to slowly move my body up and down the shaft. The first few strokes are shallow, then it is to the hilt and my breath gets knocked out of my body. My flesh shivers as my muscles clench tighter.

'You won't believe how hot and tight you feel,' he whispers, his hand sliding down my belly, and between my legs to play with my clit.

That makes me swoon. Surely I am not going to come so quickly. My body arches like a bow. I grasp his arms—the muscles are bulging with the effort of holding my body and moving it up and down his shaft. I lock my jaw as my chin lifts up, to stop from screaming. And then it comes, a liquid explosion inside me. It is powerful and totally different from any other orgasm I have experienced. It is dark and thick and flavored with something forbidden. On and on until my energy is spent.

My dazed eyes return to his eye level. His are smoldering darkly with fresh intent. His cock jerks within me as he lifts my body and drops it hard and fast on his shaft. My mouth opens involuntarily. My sated flesh purrs and comes alive again. I balance myself on his shoulder and rise to my knees. My limbs slick with sweat, I fuck him as hard and as fast as I can. The wet heat and friction are delicious.

He comes snarling my name, his seed shooting into my body, mixing with my fluids in a long, hot release. His breath is rough and ragged. I put my hand on his chest and feel his heartbeat, swift and loud. An African drum in Thailand.

'I want to go home and finish this,' he says.

My eyebrows fly upwards. 'After *that*.'

He grins. Feral. 'I want to take your bra off and suck your breasts, deep pulls that will leave you squirming and delirious.'

Not taking my eyes off his, I uncouple from his cock, making a most unladylike sucking sound. He pulls my dress over my dripping sex. Cum is still trickling out of me as we leave the nightclub.

# Twelve
## Victoria Jane Montgomery

That night I wait until it is late. I lie in my bed and watch the low-lying mist shroud the vast expanse of green outside this dreadful mad house until the phones by the nurses' station have stopped ringing. Until there is no more noise other than the odd screaming that will suddenly pierce the night. Until the lone night nurse thinks everybody is asleep and she is busy watching porn on the Internet.

Then I get under the covers and shine the little torch my mother brought me on my musical box. It is an old antique. A ballerina in a lilac tutu. The tutu is almost gray now. I touch the delicately painted porcelain face. It belonged to my great grandmother and came directly from her to me. It did not pass my grandmother or mother so they do not know about the secret compartment it conceals at the bottom of the figurine.

Carefully, I depress the lever that opens it. So many years since I opened it. It is a little sticky and I pull it, but that just jams the drawer. I come out of the covers and look for something to pull it open with. A knife or anything sharp, but there is nothing sharp in the room or the bathroom. In frustration I bang the ballerina with the side of my fist. It still will not open. For some reason this infuriates me to unreasonable anger.

I guess that is what road rage is. Someone cuts you up and you react as if someone has raped your daughter. I throw the musical box against the wall. The sound of it shattering is almost a profanity.

For a moment I don't move. I listen. No one comes. I walk toward the box. The drawer is open. I reach into it and take out the small, folded document inside.

I open it out and look at it in the light of the torch.

For a moment I remember, tangled with him, bonded skin to skin, sharing breath. The way Blake had felt deep inside me. Then I remember— that was not him. That was some other random man that crawled into my life at three a.m. Forget that.

This, this tiny piece of paper in my hand is my ticket out of here.

Blake Law Barrington, you're about to get the shock of your life. You shouldn't have double-crossed me.

# Thirteen

## Lana Barrington

It is during the end of the second act, when the Prince sings to Turandot, '*You do not know my name. Tell me my name before sunrise, and at dawn, I will die.*'

I turn away from the stage and look at Blake. His phone must have vibrated in his pocket, because he is checking the lighted screen. He smiles at me and leaves the box to take the call. It could have been anyone, calling about any number of urgent matters, but it is as if my heart already knows: the unthinkable has happened. For a moment I do nothing, simply sit terrified where I am, and listen to the cruel Turandot accept the Prince's challenge.

By dawn he will be dead.

Then I stand and follow Blake out. As I open the door I see him terminating his call. His body is stiff and tense. When he looks up at me he looks ashen. I see his hands tremble as he puts his phone away. I stare at him aghast. I was right. The unthinkable has happened.

'What's happened? What is it?' My voice sounds hollow and scared.

He starts walking toward me. 'I've called Tom to pick us up. We have to go home now.'

Fear. Fear. Fear like I have never known coils around me, crushing me so hard, I can hardly take my next breath. I know what he is going to say. I know exactly what he is going to say. I realize I don't want him to say the words. My head is shaking.

'No, no,' I whisper, and start backing away from him.

The second act is over, and all around us people in their finery are streaming out of their boxes, heading toward the restrooms and the bars. I take another backward step and collide with a man in a black suit. He steadies me with his hands. He has dirty blond eyebrows and concerned, muddy brown eyes.

'Are you all right?' he asks.

I gaze stupidly at him with my mouth hanging open.

Before my confused, frightened brain can even formulate a reply, Blake appears at my side and takes my arm. The other man drops his hands. He smiles oddly at me and with a nod to Blake leads the woman with him away. My mind reels and incongruously notes that her velvet dress has a tiny stain on the right sleeve. And yet she seems happy. She doesn't have bad news waiting for her at home. Suddenly I feel nauseated. My fingers shake as they rush to cover my mouth.

'We have to get home,' Blake mutters. He leads me through the throng of people. The bar is crowded and the foyer seems suddenly very noisy. We get outside. I take a gulp of cool evening air and shiver. My shoulder curls up around my ears and my ribcage tightens to avoid breathing in the cold air.

'You're cold,' Blake says.

'I left my wrap in the box,' I reply in a daze. As if it matters.

He takes off his jacket and wraps it around my shoulders.

I snuggle into the living warmth of his body heat and put off for another second hearing what he has to say to me.

'Sorab's missing. Looks like he's been taken.'

I nod. As if he had said to me, 'Let's have a drink before dinner.' Fighting a sense of disbelief, I clutch his jacket lapels close together and glance away from him. There's a beggar sitting on the theater steps. He has a mangy dog. It looks mournfully at me. Poor thing. Living on the streets, eating scraps. Someone's taken *my* baby. I turn back to Blake.

'How?' My voice is surprisingly flat. Almost uninterested. I am conscious that my reaction is strange, to say the least. Perhaps I am in shock.

'That's what I intend to find out. Brian thinks it's Ben.'

'Ben?' I repeat. My hands drop to my sides.

Blake nods. 'He's gone AWOL.'

'He's one of the new guys, isn't he?'

'Yes.'

I force the words out of my throat. 'One of the men you hired because I asked you to,' I whisper. My teeth have started chattering.

He pulls his jacket tightly around me and holds me close to his body. I register the heat instantly. He radiates it like a hot water bottle.

'Stop it. It's not your fault,' he says into my hair. 'Come. Tom's here. We have to go.'

I turn in the direction he is looking in and see Tom stop the car. Tom doesn't smile. He looks pale. Blake opens the door and I enter and sit down huddled inside his jacket. I can't feel anything, but a numbing cold. I clasp my fingers together in my lap to stop them from shaking. Nothing feels real.

I try to remember Ben. Dark hair, generally unsmiling with caramel eyes, suspicious caramel eyes. But that means nothing. They are all like that.

'Is it possible that Ben might have taken Sorab for a ride in his car...and just not told anyone?' Even as I say it I know it could never have transpired like that.

Blake shakes his head slowly and squeezes my icy hands.

His thigh is close but not touching mine. I shift so it is touching me and that thin stretch of contact comforts me. I stare silently out of the window, not seeing a thing, and listen to him making phone calls.

'Get the word out. I want to know who has my son.'

I place my palm on the cold glass pane. I'm so numb. Some of the one-sided conversation slips through the cold fog I am in: Something about seizing Ben's phone records. Somebody has been to his place. Looking for clues. The phones are already tapped. A police inspector has been discreetly and unofficially contacted. Feelers are already out in the street. The disjointed thought in my numb brain: how fast these men move. As if they were expecting such a scenario. An ambulance, its siren turned off, but its lights flashing, passes us on its way to another tragedy.

I think of Sorab's little face and a shudder goes through me. Where is he? He is not familiar with Ben. He will be so frightened. He will have to go to sleep without his favorite toy. He has never been to bed without clutching Sleepy Teddy. I think of him blinking up at me from my lap. The image is oddly painful.

And then a clear thought, so comforting: They will not hurt him. They just want money. Blake will give them whatever they ask. I know Blake has ties with the underworld and the mafia. Obviously, we will get our son back. Some part of me knows, of course, that I am probably deceiving myself, but at that moment that baseless belief comforts me tremendously. I lie back and close my eyes and don't allow myself to think further than that. I just listen to the blood pounding steadily in my ears and concentrate on the feel of Blake's thigh pressed into mine.

When I get home the nightmare becomes real. The dining room looks like a war office with listening equipment and gadgets I cannot recognize, and Geraldine looks at me with huge, frightened eyes.

'I'm so sorry, Lana. I was only in the toilet for a minute,' she says in a trembling voice.

# Fourteen
## Blake Law Barrington

Brian walks into the room and lowers himself into a chair and sits forward. He is sporting bronze stubble and looks uneasy. My senses flash a warning and adrenalin starts frothing into my veins. His eyes, always deliberately expressionless anyway, are flat and dead. I've known him a long time.

'You're not going to like this,' he says.

A man like him is not prone to exaggeration. In fact, he is like a black hole sucking in all kinds of information and observations and never giving anything back. At his words a strange coldness invades my body. It is already so tense that it feels as if every nerve is screaming, but I force myself not to react.

'We picked up the pings that came off the unidentified mobile phones that Ben was in contact with. We ran through every number on them for the last six months. One of the numbers was registered to a woman called Angel Levene. She works in the mental asylum Victoria is committed in. But here's the real kicker. The one time it was used to call Ben's number, the tower that served it was located close to the mental asylum.'

A chill goes through my body. I gape. 'Victoria?'

Brian doesn't say anything. A corner of his eye twitches. I never noticed that nervous tic in his cheek. I drop my eyes to the papers on my table and see a blur of white. *You're not going to like this*. It has scared the shit out of me. I'm fucking terrified.

Fruitcake Victoria's got my son? The implications are beyond anything I could have imagined.

For a long time after Brian leaves I do nothing. Simply stare out of the window. Shocked by how blissfully unaware I had been of the impending storm. Once, I would never have been caught so unprepared. I have changed. I've become soft. Then I get up and go to look for her. She is in the south facing reception room. She spends most of her time there now. The rest of the house seems so full of cold-eyed men. I can hear strains of Puccini's *Nessun Dorma* as I get closer. It makes my hair stand on end.

*Nobody shall sleep! Nobody shall sleep! Even you. O Princess.*

I stand at the door and watch her, how still she is. When I move into the room, she catches the movement and starts rising to meet me, but she is seemingly so dazed she has to test the sole of her shoe on the floor before she puts her weigh on that foot.

We stand a few feet away from each other. I'll never be able to listen to Turandot again without having this feeling that I am a falling glass, about to hit the tiles. About to shatter into a thousand pieces.

# Fifteen
## Lana Barrington

He stands at the door of the living room. He knows something. And it's not good. I stand and look at him expectantly.

'Victoria's got him.'

Time stops. I freeze. He freezes. Then I am flying across the room to him—he catches me and holds me so tightly against his chest my feet lift off the ground. I begin to sob into his neck.

'Don't, my darling. Don't cry, don't,' he whispers again and again, but I cannot stop. I want to blame someone, but there is no one to blame.

He gathers a fistful of my hair and pulls my face away from his neck and kisses me. His kiss is odd. It is as if with that kiss he wants to suck away my pain. There is no erection against my stomach. Even in my sorrow, I hate that. It feels wrong. Everything is wrong. I let the strange passionless kiss go on and on and then I break away and stare at him breathlessly.

'But you said she is locked away in an asylum?'

'She is.'

I frown. 'Then how can she...? I don't understand.'

'Victoria is more resourceful than I gave her credit for.'

So there *is* someone I can blame. I can blame him. He is at fault. It is his fault that my baby is gone. At that moment I feel his separateness from me. My face twists at my own crazy thoughts. I pull myself back from that cliff edge. But even that one second of doubt and blame that I indulge in breaks something precious. I break 'us'.

I see his face change and a look of such hurt and pain come into his eyes that I am immediately filled with regret. He has given me so much and asked for so little in return. My hands rush up to his neck and wrap themselves tightly around it.

'I'm sorry. I'm sorry, darling. I did not mean it. I love you. You're the last person I want to hurt. I'm just so scared I don't know what I'm saying.'

'But you are right. It is my fault. You entrusted me with his safety. I have failed. I have let both of you down.' His voice is scarily quiet. In all the time I have known him I have never heard it so. It feels as if he has walked away from me, for good. I pull back and stare at him. Could it be that what we had was nothing? That with one moment of mistrust he could walk away. That our great love cannot survive this tragedy.

He turns away from me, and my betrayal of him during his time of greatest need. I try to pull him back to me, but he is already striding away. I watch the door shut behind him with horror.

For some time I wait. His footsteps become fainter. I listen intently. Maybe he will realize and come back. Of course he will come. A whole minute passes. He's not coming back. When I hear his car start outside, I sink to the floor and, holding onto my belly with both hands, sob—ugly wrenching wails that come from a place I did not know existed.

I did not feel this depth of loss even when I walked away from Blake, pregnant and lost, and left for Iran. It seems as if all this while I was playing at motherhood. I have known nothing, but the fun stuff. But this—this hurts so fucking bad.

'Oh God. Oh God. Please don't take my son away from me. Please. He's just a baby. Take me.'

Suddenly, I stop blubbering. There it is. The truth that was staring me in the face the whole time. It is not Blake's fault. It is mine. I came back to Blake. I dared her wrath. I was the one who was so naïve and stupid I did not think further than my passion. Both Billie and Jack warned me and I did not listen. It's not Blake that is to blame. It is me. I stole another woman's man.

I took her money, and arrogantly, stupidly thought nothing would come of it. That there would be no consequences. No debt collectors would come a calling.

I bite my fist.

Then I find my mind clearing. There is nothing to cloud it. I have lost my son and I have lost Blake. There is not even an erection between us left.

Without lust, I see my path clearly. It is as if it is lit by a thousand lanterns. My mother stands at the end of it. It is not Sorab that Victoria wants. It is me. All I have to do is give Blake up. That's all. A sob chokes me. I am surprised by it. By the selfish instinct that prompted it. I stand. I know exactly what must be done.

Blake in exchange for my son.

Another traitorous sob rises up my throat. I swallow it down. Silent tears begin to run down my face. It is only my body making its stand. I'm not about to listen to it. I stand up and go to my bedroom. I open my jewelry box. I lift the first tray. Throw it to the ground. The second tray follows quickly. I take a cleansing breath. A breath of love. There it is. Her card. All this time I saved it. Why? Because some cautious part of me knew this day was coming.

I take it out and look at it. The truth is I don't need to look at it. Every single letter and number on it is indelibly imprinted into my memory bank.

I go to the bedside and the phone. I sniff once. Just to make sure that my voice when it comes out will be strong and sure. Then I clear my throat and cough. I pick up the phone and a voice full of pain and sorrow says from behind me, 'Don't call her, my darling.'

I turn toward the voice. My mouth parts in a soundless cry. My nose is so blocked from crying I can't breathe through it anymore. I gaze at him sadly. The truth is he is my life, and fresh tears start pouring from my eyes.

'For Sorab,' I sob.

'Not even for Sorab.'

'Why?'

'Because I will not give you up for anything.'

'He is our baby. He is innocent. He is depending on us to protect him,' I whisper.

'He is my son. I will give up my life for him, but I will not give you up and live with her for him.'

I close my eyes. If only this was all a nightmare that I could wake up from.

'Understand this, Lana. You are mine. You belong to me. Because you are young and you have never had others, you are like a child who has been given a priceless antique. You know not the price so you are willing to do the exchange. I will die before I let you make such an exchange.'

'For Sorab,' I plead.

'You still don't understand, do you? You can go on without me for Sorab's sake, but I cannot. Without you nothing makes sense. Everything is meaningless.'

I stare at him blankly. I know his words carry meaning, important meaning, but they wash over me. I made that boy in my body. God gave him to me to introduce to this world. He deserves my loyalty. Until he can fend for himself I am his mother. I will fight his corner to the end.

Blake walks towards me and stands directly in front of me. 'I know you want me to say otherwise, but I can only tell you what is in my heart. I love Sorab, but I love you more. When Sorab wants to go to summer camp, I will allow it, then I will watch with pride when he goes off to university and moves out, but you—I will not allow myself to be parted from you for one day.'

'I don't want to be parted from you either.'

'Besides there is far, far more at stake than you understand.'

I know instinctively that he is right. I know nothing about these people, their cold and brutal ways. Slowly, I replace the receiver on its hook.

'You don't understand her. Maybe I don't understand her either, but I still want you to trust me that I understand her better than you. I want you to know I would die for my son. There is no greater commitment than that. I will get him back.'

'If you don't?'

'That is defeatist thinking. Don't defeat me, Lana. You are the only one who can.'

I run into his arms. 'Just bring my son back to me.'

He pries the card from my hand, not realizing I have memorized its contents.

'Promise me only one thing.'

'What?'

'Never contact her. She will destroy you and Sorab.'

I nod.

'There is something important you must know. While you are safe he is safe.'

I nod again. I am so frightened, I am glad he is taking over. My plan was no plan at all. It was to beg pity from the criminally insane. Stupid strategy.

He looks at his watch. 'I want you to eat.'

I start shaking my head.

'You have to be strong for Sorab.'

I cover my face. 'I can't eat.'

He nods. 'Then you will watch me eat.'

He puts his hands around my waist and we walk together to the kitchen. He moves toward the refrigerator. And it occurs to me that I know exactly how I can be of use. I can keep him strong.

'I'll do it,' I say, and I open the fridge door and rummage around. The chef has left some lamb chops wrapped in cling film.

'Would you like me to make you a meal, madam?' Rita, my housekeeper, asks from the doorway. She has curly hair and wears glasses. Usually she spends her nights at her daughter's house in Surrey. She must be staying over because of the situation with Sorab.

'Thank you, Rita, but I can manage.'

'It's no problem.'

'No, I'd like to keep busy.'

She nods and disappears.

I find some broccoli and carrots to go with the chops. There is also mint sauce and some parsnip mash in a covered dish. Blake sits on an island stool while I prepare his meal for him. We do not speak.

He stares at me while I move around, but I know he is not really watching me. He is laying his plans. Once he expels his breath and says, 'OK, OK.'

I say nothing. I know he is not talking to me.

Quietly, I work. It is therapeutic. When I put his food in front of him, he picks up his knife and fork and eats automatically. There is no enjoyment or sign that he is even tasting the food. Once or twice, he frowns. Halfway through his meal he stops eating, looks at me, smiles faintly and says, 'Sometime ago I had my soul put in a box and delivered to you.'

I sit with my hands clasped on the counter.

At the end of it all, he gazes down as if perplexed at his empty plate. 'Will you be all right if I leave you alone for a couple of hours?'

I nod.

# Sixteen

I wake up suddenly from a restless sleep full of strange dreams and there is no moment of forgetfulness or mercy. Of slowly facing up to the day. The knowledge is instant and burning: my greatest enemy has my son. I close my eyes and wish again for sleep. But sleep does not come.

Instead I am filled with the terrible pain of knowing she has him. That we won't be able to simply buy our way out of this nightmare. Whether he lives or dies lies at the whim of a mad, vindictive woman. I open my eyes and stare at the ceiling. Stare with bewilderment at my darkness. I am so lost and frustrated I want to scream, but I can't.

I honestly feel as if I am losing it, going insane.

If only I had not gone to the theater. If only I had not asked Blake for more protection. If only he had not hired more men. If only I had just trusted Brian and let things be.

My head starts to ache.

Blake's hand is heavy on my stomach. Carefully I move out from under the weight. Quietly, I fumble around, locate my alarm clock and depress the light button. Two a.m.

I sit up and press my throbbing temples. God, how I long for just one minute of forgetfulness from this insistent guilt and pain. Silently, I leave the bed and go toward Sorab's room. For a long while I simply stand at the entrance looking at the empty cot. My heart is very loud in my chest. Ever since Sorab was taken I haven't dared go into the nursery. I am almost afraid of it. I press my lips together and cast my eyes along the painted walls of fluffy clouds and stars.

My gaze grazes his toys. The sight of them hurts my eyes. I cover my mouth with my hand and move my eyes away quickly to the rack of CDs. There with all his nursery rhymes is Mozart. I bought Mozart for him because I read somewhere that listening to Mozart makes an infant more intelligent. The stupid things I concentrated on. A sob rises in my throat.

Be brave, be brave, I tell myself, and close my eyes. But immediately memories start crowding into my head.

I see it again as clear as day—sitting at the table with Billie in our little kitchen. That time when I had gone to the bank to get a loan and Blake had been waiting for me. I remember that wooden table. She warned me. But I didn't listen. I was so in love, so crazy for any crumbs from Blake's table that I was blind to the danger. I traced the scratches on the table and naïvely told Billie nothing bad was going to happen. That even though I had taken the woman's money and her man she would not retaliate. Of course she was not going to go quietly.

I've been so silly, so stupid.

So unbelievably naïve.

I shake my head to dislodge the guilt, and dig deeper into myself. Courage, Lana, courage. I am determined to be brave. So I made mistakes. I will confront my demons. I will get my son back. Come back. Come back to me. I don't care what I have to sacrifice to get you back. An ugly, unwanted thought intrudes. What if it is Blake? What if it is Blake that you have to give up?

Are you prepared for that?

I walk up to the cot, shivering with the endless chill in my bones, and Sleepy Teddy's glassy eyes watch me. In the darkness he seems sinister. It is my imagination. Obviously, he is not sinister. Sorab loves him. I pick the toy up and cuddle it, and suddenly, I am enveloped by the smell of my son. It is so strong it is as if he is in my arms. A sharp pain pierces my chest and I almost cry out then. The pain is so great I drop Sleepy Teddy, and, turning around, blindly run from Sorab's nursery.

My feet are soundless on the carpet. My throat stings with unshed tears. I want to scream and howl. It will be some kind of a release, but how can I? At this time of the night? I wish I could drive out to some lonely location and scream and scream and scream. But the moment I leave the front door, Brian or one of the men will start trailing me.

I pause at the entrance to our bedroom and stand gazing at Blake. He looks very pale sleeping among shadows. I feel as if I have lost everything. I am so incredibly scared. I need to hear him call out my name in that snarling voice again. Without thinking I drift, like a flower crowned Ophelia, toward him, toward the warmth of his body. At the edge of the bed I look down on him, my eyes exploring the tousled hair, relaxed muscles, the smooth and gleaming skin. He is so incredibly sexy. But I'm not wet with desire. I want to be wet with desire again.

Carefully, I lift the duvet and crawl onto the bed next to the magnificent body. His scent is sun ripened and heady. I take his soft penis into my mouth. Slowly, gently, I suck it. He tastes delicious.

The juices begin to gather between my legs.

He moans in his sleep, his throat moves, and I increase the pressure of my mouth. The shaft grows thicker and bigger. Blake's hands come up to hold my shoulders. I don't look up. I just keep on sucking. His hands grip harder. Suddenly they are under my armpits, and pulling me up, and over his body.

'Let me finish,' I say, but already I am straddling his hips.

I move my body encouragingly, and my sex, wet and willing, rubs against the short silky hairs on his thighs. He lifts me up silently and holds my body over the head of his cock. I hold onto the shaft and position it over the core of my heat.

Slowly, my sex is stretched and fitted around that aroused throbbing shaft. He spreads my thighs even farther and flattens them against his hips. The action makes my clit touch bone. He grinds that bone against me. Then tension transfers to my belly, my thighs, my sex. My nerves overload, and soon I am lost in a red mist of forgetfulness. It explodes in my brain.

He holds me by the waist and rolls me under him. I close my eyes and let my body be a vessel for his satisfaction. For a while I am simply a body, a body that is being fucked by another body. I am nothing but a biological reaction. When I feel the first drop of water on my cheek, I think it is Blake's sweat, but when the next drop splashes onto my forehead, I know. They are tears. And then it is impossible for me to even be a biological reaction. He feels the change in me, and stops moving.

'I'm sorry,' he whispers. The words are strange in his mouth.

I grab his wet face in my hands. 'It's OK. We're not supposed to enjoy ourselves while he is not here.'

'Trust me. I'll get him back,' he says. His words are like spells in the night.

I nod quickly, my eyes filling up with tears again. He runs one finger in my hair. The action is unusual. Affectionate. We lost our passion. We have become pitiful creatures. I look at him sadly. Maybe we have lost too much to recover.

Now I understand why so many couples who lose a child break up. Because you just can't help it—the natural instinct is to turn on each other and tear each other to pieces, so that there is nothing living left to remind you of your terrible, terrible loss.

'I will find him. If it is the last thing I do,' he promises.

'I know. I know you will.' And at that moment I don't think of any other possibility. I don't think I might need to sacrifice him for my son. Because I cannot think it.

Billie is in my head. 'If Blake and Sorab were drowning, and you could only save one person, who would you save?'

'I'm not answering that. You're a wicked witch, Billie.'

And she grinned evilly.

But now the choice is upon me. I want to, I want to with all my heart choose Blake, but I can't. I just can't. The great mistake I made was when I thought of my own pleasure before I thought of Sorab's well-being. I've learned my lesson. This time I won't think of myself. I'll do what I have always done. Put the ones I truly love before me.

# Blake Law Barrington

She makes a dreadful sound, like the last rattle in the throat of a dying animal. I turn around and wrap my arms around her tightly, and feel her open mouth press into my breast bone. Her fevered breath and the odd sounds seep into my skin and chill my heart. How effectively Victoria has wounded us.

'I *will* get him back. No matter what the price,' I repeat loudly. In the darkness my voice mocks me with its blustery hollowness.

'I know that,' she says sadly.

We lie awake for hours after that. Not speaking. Simply holding each other. At four thirty a.m. I switch off the alarm clock and get up. By five a.m. I am out of the house and itching for any kind of news of my son's whereabouts.

# Seventeen
## Lana Barrington

I call Billie at eight in the morning. I don't know why I do. Billie always sleeps late. I guess I just want to hear her voice. She sounds sleepy. I know I've woken her up.

'What is it?' she says into the phone. She tries to disguise it, but there is an undercurrent of panic in her voice. She is expecting bad news. The thought that she is expecting bad news makes me feel frightened. The tears that are at the backs of my eyes surge forth.

'Nothing has happened. I just wanted to ask you something.'

'What?'

'If Sorab and I were drowning, whom would you choose?'

'I wouldn't. I'd let us all drown.'

I stare blankly at the wall. Maybe that is the right answer. Why should I choose between my husband and my son? Let us all perish if need be.

'Do you want me to come over?'

'Yes,' I sob, and put the phone down. I am a mess. I am a terrible mess. I want my son back.

The phone rings almost immediately after I terminate Billie's call. I look at it with surprise, my sobs dying in my throat. It is an unknown number. I only hesitate for a second. I don't know how I know but I know instantly that it is *her*. She is calling me. My thumb hits the answer button.

'Hello.'

'Will you come and see me?'

'Of course.'

'Bring my money with you.'

'When?'

'When you've got the money obviously.' There is a thread of amusement in her voice.

The line goes dead. I don't hang about. I call the bank manager immediately.

'I need it straight away,' I tell him.

He tries to do what he does with anyone that wants a super large cash withdrawal. He starts making excuses as to why I can't have it in the next hour. He picked the wrong woman. Coldly, in the same voice that Blake's mother uses when she wants to decimate someone, I reduce him to what he really is. An idiot puppet implementing policies that he knows are wrong and immoral.

'Listen, you spineless creep, it's my damn money and I'll damn well withdraw it when I like, or I'll terminate the entire account from your pathetic little bank. You've got twenty fucking minutes!'

I call Billie and tell her not to come over.

'Why?' she demands.

'Victoria called me. I'm going to see her.'

There is a shocked silence. 'Does Blake know?'

'No, and I'm not telling him. Not yet, anyway. This is between her and me. She's asked me to give her back her money. And I'm doing just that.'

'Are you fucking out of your mind? That crazy bitch is probably trying to make you pay for the cost of hiring the kidnappers or something.'

'Maybe,' I concede. 'But Victoria doesn't need money from me to pay off the kidnappers. She wants me there for a different reason.'

'Yeah. To gloat.'

'So let her have her satisfaction.'

'Don't go, Lana. You'll only make it worse.'

'I don't want to argue with you, Billie. I need to see her face to face. If she wants me to beg, I will. I just want my son back.'

'You're not getting your son back by begging.'

'Give up, Billie. I'm going and no one is stopping me.'

Unhappily, Billie rings off.

I put the phone down utterly steady in my resolve. You see, I may be naïve, one can even call me stupid, but what no one knows is that I am willing to give up my life for my son. In a second. So she wants to gloat? Let her gloat. Whatever makes her happy. And all the while I can't help thinking that maybe, just maybe, I will find that chink in her armor. And even if I don't, maybe I can glean some clue as to Sorab's well-being, or his whereabouts.

I don't bother to hide or be sneaky with Brian. I tell him my decision and ask him to take me to the

bank to pick up the money. He looks at me with a swift appraising glance before making a half-hearted attempt to dissuade me. Maybe he is a better judge of character than I have given him credit for, and knows that it would be a pointless exercise.

'You're playing right into her hands. She's going to use this money to pay the kidnappers off.'

I notice that he came to the same conclusion as Billie. Only he omitted the word probably. I look him in the eyes. 'I know that, but do you really think she has no other means to get her hands on the cash?'

He says nothing, but it is abundantly clear that he does not agree with my decision.

'So she wants to savor the irony of it all, or even my fall. Let her. It seems I owe her that.'

'We should tell Blake.'

I glare at him. 'If you tell Blake, consider this the last time you will ever see me.'

His eyes flash. It is wrong of me, I know. He has done nothing wrong to me, but I don't have a choice. He doesn't love my son. I do. With all my heart. Yes, Brian is loyal, very loyal, but he doesn't understand.

He drives me to her in silence. In the car Blake calls.

'Where are you?' he asks.

'I'm at home, of course,' I say. The lie drips off my tongue.

Brian doesn't bat an eyelid. Just stares ahead and carries on driving.

'Are you sure you are all right?' Blake insists.

'Yes. Yes, I am. I'll see you tonight.'

'I love you, Lana.'

'I love you too,' I say softly, and cut the call.

I turn toward Brian. 'Thank you.' My voice is full of gratitude.

He nods.

He has made his alliance. He had no real choice, but ultimately, he knew he would not have survived any betrayal of me. Nothing can be more ferocious than a mother protecting her young. Today, he has become a friend of mine. I will defend him to my dying day.

The building is grand and imposing the way that an austere, granite sarcophagus standing on a high plinth can be, until you remember the pathetic scattering of bones languishing at the bottom of it. I walk into the building quickly, the brown envelope from the bank at the bottom of my bag.

It is brightly lit and cool inside.

It is not visiting time, but at reception they are expecting me. They seem eager to please. They refer to her respectfully as Lady Victoria. It is not like a mental hospital. It is like her personal office.

A smiling nurse takes me to a waiting room. This must be the room they will bring Blake to when she summons him. I try to imagine which chair he will sit in. I pick the one farthest from the door. I sit and stare at the magazines on the table blankly. I don't know how long passes, but it seems a long time. Eventually the door opens and she enters with a nurse.

'Ring the bell when you are finished,' the nurse says to me with a smile.

I rise to my feet. Victoria has come to meet me in her hospital issued pajamas and a voluminous dressing gown. I consider that a threat. I get it. You only dress for those you want to impress. I too have not bothered to dress, but for the opposite reason. To show her that I am subservient to her. To allow her the opportunity to see how low she has brought me.

She takes the sofa opposite to mine and coolly folds herself onto it.

I sit down, and taking the envelope out of my bag, push it across the coffee table toward her.

She covers it with her hand and pockets it in her dressing gown. Her nails are cut to the quick. It must be hospital regulation.

'My, isn't this strange?' she says, looking at me without any sign of hostility.

'Yes, this is very strange.'

'You look terrible,' she notes.

'I feel terrible.'

'You should. You are a thief.'

I bite my lip. 'How is he?'

'He's a bit of a spoilt brat. He won't eat properly... And he bites.'

My heart feels as if it is breaking. I don't show it. 'He is a good boy. He is just not used to strangers.'

'And the only word the brat seems to have mastered is no.'

She is playing with me. I resist the compulsion to tell her that Sorab can say more than just no. He can say yes. He can say Daddy, Sleep Teddy, din din for dinner, and Lana. No matter how many times I try to correct him he refuses to call me Mummy.

'How is he?' I repeat.

'I wonder what you will give up for your son?'

I look at her. I know she wants the ultimate sacrifice. 'What do you want from me?'

'I haven't decided yet. I'll think about it and let you know if there is anything.' She stands up and, walking to the door, rings the bell.

What? She's leaving! I stand unsteadily. 'Victoria?'

She turns around and directs a withering look at me.

'He is just a baby,' I say, and the tears start flowing. 'Please, Victoria. I will go away. I'll walk away and stay away this time. I'll do anything you want.'

'What would be the point of that?' she sneers. 'You have already proven yourself to be a brilliant liar. You simply cannot be trusted. As soon as you have that brat back in your hands you will break all your pathetic little promises. So no, don't bother.' She turns back to the door to wait for the nurse with her back to me.

'I'm sorry,' I sob. 'I know I didn't keep my word, but I was... I was blinded by my love for Blake.'

It is the wrong thing to say. Her passive aggressive façade smashes to dust, and her head jerks around like a striking cobra. 'And what about my love for Blake?' she demands furiously. 'That counted for nothing, did it?'

'You said it was an arrangement.'

She turns around fully and faces me, eyes glittering with hatred. 'It was *not* an arrangement. And you knew that,' she spits venomously.

I stare at her, standing still, but vibrating with rage and hate. It is obviously pointless to try to reason with her. And yet, I can't stop. Not now. Not after I've come this far. 'You told Blake you understood. That he should cleanse me out of his system.'

'You're a pathetic hypocrite. Trying to justify stealing another woman's man. What he sees in you is beyond me.'

My spine straightens. 'I didn't steal him. He was not yours. He never loved you. I saved you from a loveless marriage.'

She laughs. A horrible sound: a vulture's cry as its talons grip into dead meat. 'Are you suggesting I thank you?'

'Of course not.'

She wants to claw my eyes out. I see it in her clenched fists, her scorching eyes, her heaving chest, but she controls herself with a Herculean effort, and grimaces. 'If I were you, I'd stop talking. You're not in any way helping your son's cause.'

A cold hand inside my chest. I shouldn't have come. I've made it worse. Blake was right. 'I'm

sorry. I'm really sorry for what I did. I'm begging you, Victoria. Please, give me back my son.'

'Look at you whining and crying because someone took your toy away from you.' Her voice is brutally contemptuous.

'He's my son.'

'Whatever.'

She turns away from me.

'Please give me back my son.'

She does not turn back. Simply ignores my pleas until the nurse comes to take her away. The nurse's eyes flick over my tear-stained face curiously, as she holds the door open for me. I go out with them and watch the nurse walk up the corridor together with Victoria and go through a locked door. Victoria never turns to look at me.

Filled with a sense of disbelief at how spectacularly wrong it has all gone, I turn around and walk out of the hospital. I use the back of my hand to wipe away the tears from my cheeks.

I should have practiced what I was going to say. I said all the wrong things. Why did I ever think there was even the slightest chance that I could appeal to her sense of pity? I stand at the top of the stone stairs and I see Brian standing next to the car staring at me. For a moment my head swims and my knees buckle. I look around for the railing to steady myself against, but it seems very far away so I sink down on the steps. Just in time. My head is feather-light. Brian comes running up to me.

'Are you all right?'

'This can't be real,' I whisper.

I see a flash of pity in his eyes. If only hers had flashed so. I watch him struggle to find the right words to say.

'Let me help you to the car, Mrs. Barrington?'

I shake my head. 'Can you get my husband on the phone for me?'

He takes his mobile out of his pocket and dials Blake. 'Your wife wants a word,' he says quietly and passes it to me.

'Blake,' I say and then all the words I wanted to say are suddenly ash in my mouth and I begin to weep uncontrollably. Gently, Brian pries the phone from my hand and speaks into it.

'She's just...upset.'

Even though I am sobbing loudly, some part of me understands that Blake must have asked where we were because Brian says, 'Outside the hospital. She met Victoria and returned her money.' He pauses to listen then he says, 'Of course, I'll take her home right now.'

He helps me to the car. On the way we pass Kensington, and that church where I went and sensed my mother's presence. And again at an odd hour its door is open. It is almost like it is open for me.

'Stop the car,' I cry urgently.

Brian looks me, but he doesn't immediately stop the car.

'I need to go to that church,' I explain desperately.

'OK,' he agrees, and turns the car around at the next opportunity. He stops the car, and as I go to get out, he says, 'I'm coming in with you.'

We go into the church together and he loiters by the inside of the entrance.

There is a woman, dressed all in black. She is deep in prayer and does not look up at the sound of my entrance. I walk to the front and sit on a pew. Bowing my head I get on my knees and I pray. He must hear my prayer.

'Oh Lord,' I whisper fervently. 'Help me, please. Help me. Bring my baby back to me. We made a deal. You were supposed to take care of him and I was supposed to do everything I could to help the children of the world. I have kept my word and already started my charity.' But a small voice inside my head says, Yeah, you made little baby steps, but you haven't really poured yourself into it, have you?

Brian comes to me. 'We must go.'

I stand and follow him. And then an odd thing happens. The sun must have burst through a cloud outside, for sunlight suddenly pours through the stained window and throws colored light on the floor in front of us. It is in the image of the Madonna and child. I stop and look at the beautiful image.

I look up at Brian, my face awed, as if I have just witnessed a miracle. Indeed it seems that way to me. 'Do you think it means something?'

Brian is careful. 'Maybe.'

'It's the image of the Madonna and child.'

He nods. 'Yeah, maybe.'

# Eighteen
## Blake Law Barrington

Twenty minutes after Brian lets me know that he has dropped Lana off at the house I walk through our door. I feel like I am a stringed instrument that has been tuned too tight. Any moment something could snap my control of the situation. I stand at the entrance to the living room and look at her. She is hunched and staring at a spot on the floor. She seems so small and defeated. My heart bleeds to see her so. As if sensing my presence she looks up suddenly. Her eyes are cloudy and wet. I stride across the room and envelop her in a tight hug.

'Don't ever put yourself in harm's way again,' I whisper, caressing her cheek with my thumb.

'I wasn't ever in danger.' Her voice is sepulchral.

'You don't know what she is capable of.'

She starts suddenly, her body tense. Fuck, I shouldn't have said that.

'What is she capable of?' she asks, hoarse with fear.

'She won't hurt Sorab. He is her bargaining chip.'

She sags with relief. She's falling apart in front of me and there isn't a thing I can do about it. 'Why didn't you tell me you were going?'

'Because you would have said no.'

'Damn right I wouldn't have let you go.'

'I'm sorry. I screwed up.'

'Don't be sorry. You didn't screw up. Tell me everything she said and did. It could be important.'

So we sit beside each other and she tells me everything calmly and clearly while I listen intently. When she is finished I am so furious I want to kill that mad bitch. I try my best not to show the fury.

She searches my face. 'You were right. I shouldn't have gone. Or at least I should have had a plan. I'm afraid all I've succeeded in doing is saying all the wrong things and cementing her hatred.'

I totally agree. I wish she hadn't gone, but I try to sound warm and reassuring. 'It doesn't matter. Nothing you have said or done has changed the outcome one bit. She has a plan. Humiliating you was only one small aspect.'

'Why do you say that?'

'She wants to see me tomorrow at ten a.m.'

Her eyes become enormous. 'When did she contact you?'

'She called right after you left her. So you see it was all planned. First humiliate you and then call me to the negotiating table.'

'What does she want? You?'

I curl my arm around her possessively. 'No. Not me. That would be too easy. She knows I don't give a damn about her. She wants revenge. I just don't know what that entails. Yet.'

# Twenty
## Blake Law Barrington

I walk into the red brick building and suddenly I am in a different world. I pause for a moment at the entrance. The air is cool and filled with an air of slow dreaminess, as if this place is a retreat from the dangerously busy world outside. The air of lethargy pervades the staff. They talk to me slowly and clearly—all their movements are calm and deliberate.

One of the reception staff shows me into a private room. There is a window with floral curtains, and a few low, blue-gray padded seats. A plastic coffee table with a few outdated, well-thumbed magazines.

'Someone will bring her down shortly,' she says quietly, and closes the door quietly. I walk to the window and look out. My mind is reeling. I realize I am nervous. So much is at stake. I think of how fragile Lana looked this morning when I touched her cheekbone. 'Don't think about me,' she whispered fiercely. 'Only him.'

'Hello, Blake.'

I whirl around. I was so lost in my own thoughts I did not hear her enter. For a moment I am surprised. My last memory of her is of her being held by Brian and another man while she clawed and screamed bloody murder. Now she stands before me, calm and present in a way I had not imagined. I had expected wild-eyed passion, a burning desire for revenge. Not this angel of mercy act.

'Hello, Victoria.'

She comes farther into the room and takes a seat. She is wearing a dress, blue with polka dots. It doesn't suit her. The dress rides up her thighs and she pulls it down demurely. She does not cross her legs, but sits with her knees close together. I'll admit she has me confused.

She looks up at me. There is amusement in her eyes. My God, she has taken the upper hand. I am filled with the ugly sensation that I am about to get my first lesson on how wrong I have been about Victoria. I walk to the seat next to hers. She watches me carefully. I spread myself out, lean back, rest my hands on my thighs, and fix her with an even look. I don't know if she buys my relaxed pose. I am not relaxed. I am so furious I want to punch her smiling face.

'How is my son?'

'Living in the lap of luxury.'

'If you hurt a single hair on his head you'll live to regret it.'

She crosses her legs high on her thigh, so smoothly and foxily, it takes me off guard—I don't let my eyes follow the movement, it simply registers in my vision—and smiles at me.

'I wouldn't take such an aggressive tone if I were you.'

'Why did you kidnap him?'

'Why did you have me locked up here?'

'Because you crashed my wedding and tried to slash my bride?'

'You've oversold the story.'

'Correct me then.'

'I avenged a wrong that was done to me. She stole my man and my money,' she states simply.

I feel myself flush. Shit. When I found out I should have returned her money. Such a paltry sum. 'She did not steal me away from you—'

'Liar, liar, pants on fire.'

I stare at her. 'Ours was an arrangement.'

'You cheated me.'

'I did not know how you felt.'

'And if you had?'

I shift uncomfortably.

'It would not have mattered, would it? Just like it would not have mattered to you what I felt if you had fallen desperately in love with someone else.'

'I was desperately in love. With you.'

'Look, Victoria. That is the past. I want my son back.'

'And I want you back.'

I cannot stop the horror her words provoke from showing in my face.

 136

She laughs, a cat with a mouse. 'That's not very nice.'

'What do you really want, Victoria?'

'I want out of here and I want you stripped of your Barrington seat of power.'

I frown. 'Stripped of the seat of power? Why?'

'Because you're not a Barrington.'

My blood runs cold and sluggish in my veins. I think of a snake. Winding. Untrustworthy. Feed it for a lifetime, then turn your back on it and it will bite you. 'What are you talking about?'

'Ask your mother. She'll tell you.'

'How do you know?'

'I have my ways. I knew many years ago, but I didn't care. I wanted you even if you were not a Barrington.'

I couldn't give a shit about what she thought of my lineage. I had only one objective in mind. 'If I agree to both your conditions will you return my son?'

'Of course. I have no use for the brat.'

I experience a flash of anger. Bitch. Can't let my anger make me careless. I flex my tense shoulders. My voice is calm. 'How do we do this?'

She reaches forward suddenly, swift as a snake, fixes her eyes on me, and lightly strokes my knuckles. It is like a lover's sweet touch. I freeze: the revulsion is incredible. I fight down centuries worth of instinct. The kind that saved prehistoric man from becoming the saber-toothed tiger's lunch. I stare into her eyes. She smiles sensuously.

Seems almost drunk with the power she has over me.

'I want your fall from grace to be public. I want you to give up every claim you have on the Barrington wealth. And then I want you to come here and sign me out.'

'Why? What benefit to you?'

She shrugs. 'Satisfaction.'

'Done.'

She frowns. 'Did you understand what I said? You will retain neither the name nor the wealth of the Barrington family.'

'Perfectly.'

Twisted anger flashes in her eyes. Did she actually imagine I would sacrifice my son to keep the Barrington name?

'You'd do that for her and that...little, common spawn of hers?' she lashes out with frustration.

'That little, common spawn is *my* son.'

She leans back and with pretended casualness looks at her nails. 'How wrong I was about you. I thought even though you weren't a real Barrington you were better than an ordinary commoner.' She fixes me with her eyes. 'But you're not. You are just like them. And you proved it by falling in love with the lowest scrounger of them all. You only know to put your own selfish lust ahead of truly important things.'

I stand and look down on her, an empty shell animated by hatred and intense jealously. 'I'll come by when everything is done.'

'And oh! For dinner tonight I'd like black cod with a medley of Oriental vegetables. All steaming hot and prepared by a Michelin starred restaurant.'

I look at her evenly. 'Would you like wine with it?'

She smiles. 'Yes, and I'd like a gourmet dinner delivered to me for the rest of my stay here.'

'I'll get Laura to arrange it.'

'Goodbye, Blake.'

I ring the bell to call the nurse and turn to look at her. 'If you renege on your word, I swear I will tear you apart limb from limb with my bare hands and a blunt knife.'

She laughs, an insolent, taunting laugh.

The nurse comes and I leave her poisonous presence with relief.

# Twenty-One
## Victoria Jane Montgomery

I watch him leave and feel a tingle of power sizzle right through me. His cheeks had colored. He had blushed. For the first time since I have known him I made the great Blake Law Barrington flush with shame.

I hold the power now.

I lean back. I know the drill—wait here until a nurse comes to fetch me back to my room. The door opens, and someone comes in, but it is not a nurse. A small, deathly pale man dressed entirely in black enters. His shoes are polished to a high shine. I stare at him with surprise.

For a moment my body freezes in fear. I swallow down that spike of fear, that unreasonable dread that he seems more a corpse that some mad doctor decided to animate so he may still walk the earth than an actual living, breathing human being. Revulsion and horror crawl in my blood. It is impossible to properly describe his bizarre appearance. His nose is sharp and narrow and his mouth is thin and downward turning, but it is his eyes that are the most sinister. They are red-rimmed and the irises black, shiny, empty.

As soon as those eyes connect with mine I feel a dark chill go through me. I have seen eyes like that before... I have never seen him in my life before, but I recognize him.

Unsteadily I stand and curtsy on one knee. It is not necessary, but I do it to ingratiate myself. I need allies. And allies like him are powerful, they are El sent.

'Lady Victoria.'

'At your service.'

He smiles cordially and as he comes closer to me, I start to feel almost faint. The malevolence of his presence is so palpable that my body instinctively recoils. Unable to stop myself I take a step back and to cover my reaction I pretend that I am heading for a seat and collapse on it. Not as elegantly as I would have liked. Then I busy myself with crossing my legs and arranging my skirt around me as I compose my face into lines of submissive helpfulness.

I am frightened of him. Then I remember the phoenix. Why should I fear? I am divinely guided. I am doing El's work. I have nothing to fear and yet my mouth feels like it is full of soot. I swallow the blackness and lick my lips.

'May I?' he drawls. He knows the effect he has on me...and secretly relishes my distress.

'Of course. Please.'

He sits. The movement is so deliberate and theatrical it is almost gay. But he is not. His tastes

are eclectic. I know that without knowing him. He is a sadist. One look in his eyes and I see it.

'Do they treat you well here?'

'Yes, thank you.'

'That pleases me. I asked for...helpful assistants.'

'Yes, they have all been very helpful.'

He nods. 'It won't be long before you are out.'

I don't say anything. I am suddenly afraid. I am wondering why he is here. He is not an ally of mine. He is here for a different reason.

'Who are you?' I splutter.

'We are descended from the light, the fallen light. Ah, but in fact, you are actually wondering why I am here.'

'It did cross my mind.'

'It is important to us that you have your satisfaction. Blake should pay for...cheating you. We like your little plan to dethrone him. He is not a Barrington and he should not masquerade as one, but we ask that Blake and his family come to no harm.'

I feel confused. I wanted to offer Blake as a sacrifice to the phoenix. I wanted to watch his beautiful blue eyes fading, fading. Dead. Damned forever.

He cuts into my thoughts. 'Let us remain merciful.'

'What makes you think I want to hurt him?'

'Lady Victoria, you underestimate us. It is not an attractive quality. Do not repeat the mistake. You are categorically denied permission to harm

Blake or his son. He will provide the tools of his own demise.'

To cover my frustration I bow my head. 'What do you seek?'

'Power, obedience and access.'

'You have all three with me.'

His bloodless lips stretch in a parody of a smile. Cold is what cold-blooded does. 'Good. What may seem to you like chaos is a carefully coordinated attack. The outcome will follow the design no matter what you do.' He looks to the window, beyond our conversation, to the overcast sky.

I frown with confusion. The brotherhood is rigorously selective. Blake is not a bloodline. 'What do you want with a bastard and his little mongrel offspring?'

'Unlikely alliances can sometimes be the most productive,' he says cryptically.

The door opens and a nurse comes in bearing a glass of water on a tray. I look up at her almost gratefully. Just having another person in the room even for a few seconds allows me to compose myself a little.

'Here you go,' she says, and places the glass on the low table.

'Thank you,' he says quietly.

She walks out of the door and it closes after her. I watch him pick up the glass, raise it to his pale lips and take a sip. I watch the movement his thin throat makes. My eyes are drawn to his Adam's apple. The skin there is so white and stretched so tight it almost glows.

My thoughts whirl in circles. Sucking at me. What the hell? Must I stand by and watch Blake and his harlot prosper...again? I shake my head. Something is not right.

'Why? Why do you care so much about a non-bloodline?'

And suddenly his eyes—there is no other way to put it—become alive, as if he was a shell and someone or something had suddenly come into his empty body and animated it. I feel inexplicably exposed and observed, not by passive eyes but by penetrating ones. Eyes that know me. Eyes that are familiar. My hand comes up to my throat. Those cruel lips hardly move, but what comes out of them turns my whole world upside down.

# Twenty-Two
## Blake Law Barrington

So it was all a lie. I am not a Barrington. Not a bloodline. Not precious. Not better than all the rest of humanity. It should have been a terrible blow. I should have been numb with shock, or in a rage. My whole life a lie! It's a strange thing but walking away from Victoria, I feel oddly light and relieved.

Finally, it all makes sense.

My father's sweaty male skin pressed against my half bare back.

Because he was not my father. The vein of cruelty was not normal. He was my keeper. When I examine it deeper it is not relief, but a kind of dangerous excitement. As if a door that I thought would never open for me has suddenly opened. A new life stretches out for me. Within my grasp. I only have to play my cards right.

But I don't trust her. I believe she will not be satisfied with such a weak revenge. She'll want blood. It is our way. Blood to feed the gods. Probably mine. She knows she won't get away with spilling any of Sorab's. Her plans must include my death. What a pleasure to turn Lana into a widow.

The first person I call is my lawyer.

'Jay, get back to me on the fastest, most efficient way for me to cut all financial ties with the Barrington wealth.'

There is a moment of shocked silence.

'Um… I didn't quite get that. Can you explain in more detail what you mean?'

'Let's say my brother discovers that I am not a Barrington—what paperwork would he draw up to cut me out of the fortune?'

'Right… Uh…I'll…um…have to get back to you on that.'

'Call me as soon as you know.'

'Right, yes, yes I will.'

I call my secretary and tell her to make arrangements for me to fly to New York that day. Then I call my brother.

'Marcus. I need to speak to you. I'll be there in about ten hours. Can you clear your diary for me?'

'Is everything OK?'

'Not really. But I'll tell you everything when I see you.'

After that I call Billie to ask her if she will come and stay with Lana that night. She sounds out of breath, as if she has been running up a flight of steps or having wild sex, but she not only took my call, she also agrees immediately. With that sorted, I dial my mother's number.

Nine and a half hours later I am sitting in my brother's mistress's flat. Nadia is out, and he was close by. I lower myself into a brand new white sofa and look around curiously. It is an odd place. In fact, I think it is the most unlived-in place I have ever been in throughout my life. There is not a spot of dirt, anywhere. It is just white—cold and soulless.

'Like a drink?' he asks.

'What've you got?'

He holds up a green bottle that he bought at an auction in Bonhams, London. A Special Liqueur Whiskey, from the Glenavon Distillery in Ballindalloch, Scotland. The distillery ceased production in the 1950s. He pours us two glasses of pale gold liquid, and crosses the extraordinarily white carpet to hold a glass out to me. I thank him and take a sip. The two-hundred-and-sixty-year-old smoky liquid slides down my throat tasting of copper pot stills, oak barrels, peat moss, and its own smooth patina. All the people who made it are dead. I only feel the bite when it splashes into my empty stomach and burns.

Marcus drops into a pristine sofa opposite me. 'So what's going on?' So close to me his voice echoes in the disconcertingly empty place.

I take another sip of his fine whiskey. 'Just found out today that I'm not a Barrington.'

His jaw drops. Well, at least I know now that he didn't know. 'What?'

'Yeah, apparently I'm not a Barrington.'

He recovers fast, I'll give him that. He snaps his mouth shut and goes silent for a bit while all kinds of thoughts pass through his head and flash across his eyes. All of them self-serving. 'Who told you?'

'Victoria.'

His eyes narrow. Disappointment? 'Isn't she in an asylum for the insane?'

'She had DNA results.'

He leans forward, his eyes gleaming. He looks like a man who can hardly believe his luck. I haven't seen this side of him. 'Have you...verified the results?'

'No need to. I always knew I was different.'

He leans back. His voice is dry. 'You weren't different. Quinn was different.'

'Anyway, the reason I'm here is because I want to walk away from being a Barrington heir. I want you to take over my portfolios and generally find a replacement for me in the Barrington hierarchy. The only thing I will retain are my own personal investments and Quinn's portfolio.'

He looks at me strangely, suspiciously. Once, I called this man my brother. Today I am about to see his real face. 'Why?'

'It's a long story.'

'I've got hours to kill,' he says languidly.

I explain what happened so far and as I speak Marcus exhales slowly, looks into his whiskey, shoots it, and goes back to the sparkling chrome and glass bar. He lets his glass hit the surface too loudly and winces. He sloshes whiskey carelessly into the glass, spills it on the gleaming surface. He

brings the glass blindly to his lips, takes a sip and swallows. He is drunk on my misfortune.

'Any lawyer worth his salt will tell you—any contract you sign under duress can be easily declared null and void.'

'That's just the thing. I want out.'

'What do you mean when you say you want out?' he asks casually. As if I could be spooked into changing my mind.

'I'm walking away from it all.'

He takes a large gulp, swallows and coughs. 'All?'

'All.' I stare at him curiously. Was I once like this? Was nothing ever enough for my insatiable lust for more? 'Well, anything that is not already in my name,' I confirm.

He makes a disbelieving sound. 'You'll be a pauper.' But I notice that he is not trying too hard to persuade me, otherwise. Simply gauging how serious I am.

'Hardly.'

'Well, you know what I mean.' There. There is that self-serving smile again.

'Yes, by your standards, I will.'

'Then you'll need a job. You can run the business for me.'

Strange, how I never saw the supercilious arch of his eyebrow, that condescending tilt of his chin. For the first time I see what my father or rather my stepfather saw. A greedy, grasping man of dissolute tastes who can't even pretend to lead. A spineless fool without even a whiff of what it takes to sit at the front of a dynasty as vast and powerful as the Barrington's.

I smile. 'No. I'd like to strike out on my own. Do something different.'

'You sound like Quinn.'

'You'll manage.'

'I really need you, Blake. I'll make it worth your while.'

I look at him and I am glad that he is not my brother. He wants to hire me as his employee. 'Sorry, Marcus, but I'm sure you'll forge new alliances.'

'You're just going to walk away from it all?' He is pleased with his good luck, but seems angered and irritated by my decision not to work for him. Later, when he is at the bottom of the bottle, it might occur to him to make it all legal as soon as possible.

I shrug. 'Yeah.'

He frowns, genuinely confused. 'Why?'

'When I was younger, the idea that all of nature—humans, animals, flowers, trees, mountains, rivers, galaxies, even universes—is nothing more than self-replicating fractals of an interactive biological software program based on golden ratio or the Fibonacci spiral was depressing. We are all animated mathematical constructs of great precision. It took the magic out of creation. I understood I was in a geometric prison, but I didn't know how I could escape it. Until recently. Now I find new beauty and astonishment whenever I act out of autopilot.

Whenever I leave the hive mentality, stop being a predator or lead a life of love and harmlessness.'

'Because of her?' he asks, his voice edged with some deep rage.

Ah, that's where the irritation comes from. He is envious of what I have with Lana. 'Don't go there, Marcus,' I warn, watching him over the rim of my glass.

# Twenty-Three
## Blake Law Barrington

"
How often have I said to you that when you have eliminated the impossible, whatever remains, however improbable, must be the truth? We know that he did not come through the door, the window, or the chimney. We also know that he could not have been concealed in the room, as there is no concealment possible. When, then, did he come?"
—Sherlock Holmes, *The Sign of the Four* (1980)

My mother lives overlooking Central Park in an apartment that takes up three entire floors. The ceilings are twenty-three feet high, the windows are ceiling to floor, and the endless views are quite literally breathtaking. Darkness has already fallen and the city lies a glitzy carpet of lights below me. I gaze down at the beautiful sight and feel crumpled and jaded.

A maid brings sage tea flavored with honey and warm brioches filled with foie gras and bacon curls. By the time my mother makes her fantastically elegant entrance, I have already been cooling my heels for fifteen minutes. I turn around to watch her sweep dramatically into the room, porcelain white, blonde and flawless, and remember her, when she used to dress in floor-length evening gowns and was what you would call an all-star beauty. Among other things she wore coats made out of ocelots. The memory leaves a hollow feeling in the pit of my stomach.

She smiles ruefully. 'Have I kept you waiting long?'

My mouth twists. 'Not at all.'

She sinks languidly onto a sofa, and after dutifully kissing either side of her smooth and perfumed cheeks, I take the seat opposite hers. She curls her fingers delicately into a half fist and lifts it to her mouth to conceal a sigh. Everything about her is designed to disguise the predatory gleam in her eyes.

'There is a Byzantine church in Syria, called The Heart of the Almond. Imagine such a name for a church.'

'Did Marcus call you?'

'What do you think?'

'Well, are you going to tell me who my father is? Or are we going to discuss obscure churches in Syria?'

She thinks for a moment, her eyes secretive slits of blue. 'Have you ever dreamed of a bird or an animal with glowing red eyes?'

I am unprepared for the question. If I had, my reaction would have been totally different. I would have schooled my expression. But as I wasn't, she saw the unguarded expression of shock. Even though I shake my head, she pins me with her eyes, suddenly avid and glittering with excitement.

'You have, haven't you?'

Why she would be pleased about such dreams, I don't know, but I consider them nightmares. Since I was a boy I have been trapped in dreams where I am being chased by a massive black horse with red eyes. It chases me through open fields, I can hear it snorting and breathing hard on my heels. Sometimes I will make it into an abandoned house or barn and I will lock myself in there and cower while the horse thunders its hooves at the door. Petrified, I will stare at the door as it rattles and shakes. That is usually when I wake up in a cold sweat.

'Do you know how lucky you are?'

Lucky? I am robbed of all words.

'That is the ultimate goal. To allow the master to inhabit our souls. Your father allowed it.' Her eyes become misty with the memory. 'Sometimes you could see Him looking out of his eyes. He would look out at you, alive and living, in a human form. It is the thing we do for Him. We allow him to walk the earth in human form. It is why we keep our bloodline pure. If we sully it by mixing our blood with impure lines he will no longer be able to possess us. It is the reason we have all this power. It is our reward. Ultimate power over all of mankind.' Her voice changes, becomes wheedling.

'You don't know what it feels like. You must allow him to take you over.'

I stand and take a few steps away from her. 'But I'm not a bloodline, am I?'

She laughs suddenly. The sound is sarcastic and taunting. 'You're a fool, Blake. I never imagined you would be so blind. Can't you guess that your bloodline is by far purer than the Barrington bloodline?'

I stare at her with surprise. My chest feels as if it is on fire. 'Who is my real father?'

'Do you really need me to spell it out for you?' She seems genuinely surprised that I don't know.

'Yes, God damn it,' I say harshly. 'Spit it out.'

'Your biological father is Hugo.'

'Hugo?'

'Yes, Hugo Montgomery.'

Hugo Montgomery! For a moment nothing makes sense. Time stops. The whole world outside my mother's living apartment ceases to exist. We are splendidly isolated and perched high in the sky. I stare at her. She stares back with an expression remarkable only for its lack of emotion. Her eyes are indifferent blue stones. Then the antique clock on the mantelpiece above the seventeenth-century fireplace starts again.

'What?' I ask incredulously.

'It's not that startling, surely?' she sighs.

'But he's Victoria's father!'

'Of course.'

'Victoria is my sister?'

'Half-sister.'

'I was supposed to marry her?'

'Which you didn't do,' she reminds in a silkily bored tone.

'It would have been incest if I had,' I counter angrily.

'I never suspected you of being tedious.'

'Why did the families want us to marry?'

'For the bloodline. In your offspring would have run the purest blood of all.'

'Does Victoria know?'

Her voice is very dry. 'I believe she is still recovering from the shock of it even as we speak.'

'Does Hugo know?'

She nods.

'And... Father? Did he know?'

She looks at me disdainfully, and I marvel at her heartless, carefully expressionless mask. She is like one of those nimble mountain goats. Even on the most precipitous crags she never loses her nerve or her footing. She moves so casually yet so surely as she nibbles on tufts of grass among dangerously loose rocks.

'We all did,' she exclaims. 'You didn't imagine I had a sordid little affair with Hugo, did you? We planned it and we executed it for the good of the family.'

'My God! You're all mad.'

'Madness is a subjective thing. At any rate, it would appear we failed, wouldn't it?'

# Twenty-Four
## Lana Barrington

Julie comes to see me.

She hugs me. 'I'm so sorry, Lana,' she says.

But I am hollow-eyed. I don't give a damn about people being sorry that my son has been taken from me. I want what I don't have. I want information. I want to know what Vann has told her.

I offer her coffee and she accepts. We sit next to each other drinking coffee.

'Blake will get him back,' she tells me.

I put my cup down. 'How do you know that?' I ask.

She is not daunted by my question. 'Because I understand what you do not.'

'What? What do you understand?' I demand, both my voice and manner more aggressive that I intended.

'I know that Blake is special. Once when you were not there I saw him interact with someone that Vann said is very frighteningly powerful. He didn't give an inch, and yet that frighteningly powerful man bowed to Blake. He has something they covet, Lana. They want or more likely need him. They will never let anything happen to him or Sorab.'

I look at Julie. 'You know their agenda, don't you?'

She nods unhappily.

'Tell me what it is?'

She looks at me with pity in her eyes. 'Oh, Lana. Blake does not tell you because it will grieve you.'

My fist connects with the table, so hard the coffee cups rattle. 'Do you think anything you tell me will grieve me more than what I already feel?'

She looks me in the eye. She is brave. I'll give her that. A lot braver than I gave her credit for. 'There is always room for more grief.'

I crumple in shame. 'Blake believes I am weaker than I am. I want to know.'

'I hassled Vann for ages. I wanted to know. And in the end he told me and now I am not the same. I wish I had not asked. I wish I didn't know.'

'Why?'

She looks at me sadly. 'Because there is not a single thing I can do about it.'

'I'm not a child. I deserve to know.'

But Julie just shakes her head. 'Trust Blake, Lana. He truly loves you. Everything he does is to protect you.'

I lean back in frustration. 'OK, OK. Forget I asked. The truth is, I don't care. I just want Sorab back.'

'And you will,' she says with total conviction. Conviction I wish I had.

By the time Billie arrives with a bottle of vodka, Julie is gone. She doesn't say anything, simply finds two large water glasses and fills them up, spilling quite a bit. I can see that she is already more than half sloshed. She comes to the table where I am sitting and pushes a glass toward me. I shake my head.

'Didn't think you were afraid of a little vodka,' she slurs.

Oh, what the hell! She's right. Maybe this will help dull the pain. I take the glass and start drinking it like it is water. I can see Billie's eyes widening.

Halfway down the glass, I have to stop. I feel sick. I put the glass down and look at Billie. 'This is not going to help.'

'You're strung up tight like a bow. You need to loosen up.'

'Loosen up? For what?'

'It's not your fault,' she says.

'What, no flip remark! You're losing your touch, Billie.'

'Um, yeah. Maybe.' She looks sheepish.

I take a deep breath. The alcohol is already singing in my head. But I don't feel any happier. In fact, I feel a bit sick. I put my head in my hands. 'I don't feel so good, Bill.'

'Did you eat today?'

'No, not yet.'

'Oh shit. Do you want something to eat now?'

'No.'

'Come on, I'll put you to bed for a bit.'

In my bedroom I fall on the bed and lie on my side and groan.

'Fuck, Billie, the room is spinning.'

'It's not really.'

I close my eyes and I feel Billie lie down beside me.

'I miss that kid,' she says and hiccups.

My heart does a little somersault. 'Me too.'

'He has the clearest, sweetest eyes. You could dive in and drown in them.'

'Yeah.' I smile to think of them. 'I think of them as pieces of sky boiled down to fit into his irises.'

'And he has this great cartoon chuckle.'

'Cartoon chuckle? He has a great laugh.'

'Oh God, don't you go all "my son's poo's a better color than yours" on me now.'

My laughter is both drunken and sad.

'I never wanted children until Sorab,' she says.

That sobers me. We are both silent for a while. My limbs feel heavy and my head feels odd.

'What the hell am I doing, Billie? Getting drunk at a time like this?'

'Nothing. It was a bad idea of mine. Just go to sleep.'

'Big stinking pile of smug. That was me.'

'Stop it.'

'Things between me and Blake are not good.'

I feel her body stiffen. 'Did you argue?'

'No. That's just it. All the passion is gone from our relationship.'

Her body relaxes. 'You're a silly muffin, Lana,' she chuckles.

'You don't understand, Bill,' I insist.

'When he comes back tomorrow, tell him you went to bed with me and we'll see how far banker boy's passion has fallen.'

I feel her hand come around my waist and her body spooning mine. Her big new boobs push into my back. They feel warm and firm and not uncomfortable. 'Thanks, Billie,' I mutter and wriggle closer to her. Almost immediately I feel myself slipping into sleep.

Hours later I feel Billie's hand being removed and I half-open bleary eyes. My head is throbbing. Blake smiles at me.

'You're home early,' I mumble.

'And what a lucky thing I am.' He carries me to the spare room, tucks me under the duvet and climbs in beside me.

'Nobody gets to sleep with my little angel except me,' he whispers and spoons my body exactly as Billie had.

# Twenty-Five
## Victoria Jane Montgomery

I lie on my bed and look at the moonless night and desperately wish the phoenix would come to me. There is no more peace for me since I found out that Blake is my half-brother, and I can't have the revenge I had so carefully planned. When I think of what he has done to me, my blood boils.

Once I loved him. Now I want nothing more than my revenge. I keep dreaming that I am pouring boiling oil into Blake's bitch's belly button. She screams like crazy as her skin peels and her flesh and fat bubbles and cooks like a piece of steak on a grill.

God, I hate her so much.

If only the phoenix would come again to me. I can ask it for its blessing. For I am frightened. I feel that something strange is happening to me. I hear the sounds of knives being sharpened in my head and I'm afraid I am losing my grip on my sanity. Perhaps it is because I am locked up here with all these crazies that I am becoming one too.

There are voices in my head now.

Every day these disembodied voices grow stronger and more relentless. They madden me with their harsh cackles and calls for revenge. They want blood. Blake's blood. I no longer dare attend group sessions. Fortunately, the policy here is that it is not compulsory. I dare not talk to anyone. What if I lose control and one of the voices takes over?

All of a sudden I hear a voice, a sweet, lost child voice. The questing innocence beguiles me, irretrievably draws me to her. She is in direct contrast to the usual threatening, sordid, obscene, and often downright menacing voices I am forced to listen to. I listen out for the unspoiled new voice and realize that all the other voices seem to have hung back.

The lovely new voice thrusts forward eagerly. I embrace it with all that I am. Perhaps I will be all right. Perhaps this new voice will keep me safe and guide me to the right path. Perhaps the phoenix sent this voice to me. Immediately I feel stronger.

*You can't trust anybody*, it says in its uniquely fresh and wonderful voice.

I nod enthusiastically.

*And you can't give up on divine plans.*

I nod again.

*The phoenix has sanctioned them.*

Of course the phoenix did. I listen intently as the beautiful voice elaborates on what must be the truth of the matter.

*Blake must die just as you planned—a car crash on his way home from the hospital after signing over all his rights to the Barrington fortune. Then it will be the turn of his bastard child to die.*

*Afterwards, as planned, we will pay a little visit to the lying, cheating, cock-sucking cunt he married...and watch her die, slowly and painfully.*

# Twenty-Six
## Blake Law Barrington

She comes toward me, her eyes huge, her face pale and drawn, and I feel a stab of guilt. When I found her she was bursting with life, an innocent thing in an orange dress. Look how careless I've been. Look what I've done to her.

'What is it?' I ask, holding her. She seems so small, her bones so breakable. She was not always like this, was she? No. Once she fought me on her terms.

'Blake,' she calls.

'What is it?'

She swallows hard.

'Tell me?'

'Oh, darling. You don't really want me anymore, do you?'

'What?'

'I know you love me, but you don't desire me anymore.'

I shake my head. I will never understand women. How they can be so intuitive and so dense at the same time. I run a finger down her beautiful, beautiful nose to her plump lips. I remember the first time we kissed. I remember how they looked when that fucking pervert abused her at the party. I remember them when she was laughing at that drug dealer party she invited me to, and I remember them when she told me on our honeymoon that she was my captive slave. Seems so long ago. So much has happened. I wish I could go back. I can't. Here and now is what I have.

'Lit matches,' I whisper.

'What?' she asks.

'That night I met you I thought your eyes were like lit matches. So blue. The impression of something cool and yet it'll burn your fingers.'

She bites that plump lip. 'Have I burned you?'

'Never.'

'I'm so confused, Blake.'

'Come here. I want to tell you something.' I lead her to the sofa. We sit together, our thighs touching. If only she knew. Maybe I need to spell it out to her. Maybe I've been too distant. It's my upbringing. Stiff upper lip. Better in than out.

I take her hand. It's cold. I grasp it between my palms.

'Your hand is warm,' she murmurs.

I smile at her.

'Tell me the truth, Blake. I can take it.'

'Oh, Lana. Tell you the truth? Here's the truth. Right now, I want to fuck you until you can't remember your name.'

Her head jerks. She didn't expect that. Of course not.

 166

'The only thing that stops me is your grief. I don't want my method of dealing with grief to intrude on yours.'

'What do you mean?'

'I mean the only time I forget that Sorab is gone is when I am inside you. That is the only time I don't feel the guilt that I did not protect him. I did not protect you. I let my guard down. I was careless, Lana. I didn't see her as she really was.'

'So you still want me?'

I gaze at her. In time we will learn everything there is to know about each other. For now I will just have to show her. I take her hand and put it on my groin. It is hard and throbbing for her.

Tears gather in her eyes and roll down her cheeks.

'What's the matter?'

'I really, really thought you had gone off me.'

'Gone off you? Are you totally blind? There is no one else for me. From the day we met again at the bank I have never looked at another woman. Let alone wanted one. You're the only one for me. I could take you right now if I thought you were up for it.'

She looks at me with her big, electric blue eyes. 'I'm up for it.'

I take Sorab from my head and store him safely in my heart and I start to unbutton her top.

I drink her in. Glazed doe eyes, flushed cheeks and reddened lips. Oh yes. That's my Lana. Her hands go to the front of my trousers and find me hard as a rock.

I smile. 'See? Nothing has changed between us.'

'Oh, how I've missed your body,' she whispers as I lift her up.

Her legs wrap around my body tightly. I can feel the wetness between her legs seeping into my clothes. Damp spot on my shirt. It's a good feeling.

'I was so afraid your passion was gone.'

'I can't imagine what gave you such an idea.'

'I don't want you to be gentle.'

'I didn't plan on being gentle. It's going to be as hard and dirty as they come. If you don't shatter then you're going to pass out,' I warn, swooping down to crush that plump mouth that I bought another lifetime ago. Once when I was king of the entire realm, for as far as the eye could see.

# Twenty-Seven
## Lana Barrington

Jack calls me. For an instant his voice confuses me. It seems so near. As if he could pop around for a coffee.

'Oh, Jack,' I breathe. 'Where are you?'

'In Africa. Billie emailed me. Is there anything I can do?'

'No. No, there is nothing you can do. Blake has it covered.' My voice is bitter. 'Turns out Victoria took our son to punish us.'

'I can't hear you properly. Who took him?'

'Victoria.'

'Who?

'Blake's ex?'

There is a shocked silence as he assimilates this fact. 'I thought she was locked up in an asylum.'

'She is.' I suddenly feel tearful. In my peripheral vision I see a yellow Post-it pad. It has the faint indentation of the message on the note that was above it.

'Then how can she?'

'It's called money and privilege.' I open a drawer and take out a pencil and start to lightly

run the lead over the message. A sentence in Blake's handwriting starts appearing.

Jack sounds bewildered. 'What happens next?'

'She wants Blake to renounce his inheritance.'

There is an electric pause. The line crackles with it. 'Is he going to?'

'Yes. Yes, he is.'

I hear him breathe a sigh of relief and then uncomfortable words start pouring out of my receiver. 'Thank God. It's not that I doubted him, it's just—'

'Don't worry, Jack,' I interrupt. 'They are a cold, calculating bunch and I don't blame you for thinking that.' I hold the note up and look at the message.

'I'm coming back.'

'Don't, Jack. You can't help.'

'No, I'm coming back because I'm of no use here.'

'What do you mean?'

'I'll tell you when I get back.'

'You're not in any trouble, are you?'

'No. I just realized I'm doing more harm than good.'

'All right, tell me when you get back.' In my mind another sentence forms. After I get Sorab back. But I don't say it. It's unnecessary. As unnecessary as saying I miss kissing the wet crown of my son's head as I lift him out of the bath. The real pain, the deep pain is in my bone. Hidden in the marrow. A ravenous thing, eating relentlessly, eating up the cells that hold me up.

When I put the phone down I tear away the Post-it note. The scrawl reads:

**The real target has to be me!**

I look in the mirror. My eyes look frozen over.

# Twenty-Eight
## Blake Law Barrington

'Wars should be directed so that the nations on both sides should be further in our debt.'
—Amschel Mayer Rothchild, Frankfurt 1774

I swipe my hand on the steamed-up mirror and look at myself. My eyes stare back, a hard blue. I blink. I look the same. The corruption and the ugliness don't show, but surely I must be morphing into something unspeakably ugly. All my life I have manipulated laws and morals to advance myself and those of my class.

It was all real simple. Fake money, built upon fake money, built upon fake money. We stole it all from right under your noses. How? Simply seize control of the top of any organization and the rest... You followed like sheep.

You were so easily led, so wonderfully predictable. So lacking in vision. Like a herd moving blindly, either with fear or hatred. It was all so easy. Placate the deliberately dumbed down masses with entertainment. Hundreds of channels of mush and the mindless instructions to consume, consume, consume. Like an addict you saturated your minds with violence, pornography, greed, hatred, selfishness and incessant bad news.

Then... Oh look...a terrorist. He's coming for you.

Let's put the whole world on militarized high alert. Let's intimidate!

And you rose to the bait. Or did you just look the other way?

Yeah, it was grotesque. But you bought it. Even now you're content with your subjugations, right? Your illusions of security. Are your eyes glazing over? That's why it was easy. *You* made it easy. Yes, you. Feel the spike of shame? No? See, why it was so easy for me.

Anyway...

One day, I went one step further. I killed a man, one I called Father. Struck Daddy fatally when he least expected it. And now I am being called upon to execute my sister. And still I do not flinch. Is it because I woke up this morning and the pillow under my cheek was damp? I had cried in my sleep. Or is it simply because I am a monster, a sociopath? Or is it rather just the law of the jungle?

Eat your opponent before he lays his table.

I am of the jungle. I saw her setting her table. I saw it in her eyes. That flash of raw, vindictive hatred teetering on hysteria—unmissable.

Once she fooled me. I mistook calculated revenge for hurt and deep sadness, even madness, but now I am older and wiser. I am a husband and a father and woe betide anyone who threatens harm to my little family.

This time I got her number. Yes, she will return Sorab, but that will not be enough for her. She is baying for my blood. Perhaps even theirs. No, when I think about it, her revenge will only be complete when I am dead, and Lana is a struggling widow that she can play with. And she will.

Like a cat with a mouse.

There is no other way around it. I played softly, softly with her, but she will have none of it. Now the kid gloves come off.

When she looked at me, she was not looking at her lost love, but at a piece that stubbornly refused to conform to desire, to meld with her. It was as if I was a part of her that had been denied her and she wanted it back. She wanted it like mad. Until she has subjected me in whatever way her sick mind deemed would complete her she will not stop.

Unless I rehash an old battle.

Unless I stop her.

By killing her…

I leave the bathroom and go looking for my wife. She is in the room she has designated as her new office. She is on the phone and I stand at the entrance watching her. In the last two days some change has come over her. Suddenly she seems to have thrown herself into her charity.

'Yes, I understand. But we really don't need them,' she says, and puts the phone down.

I raise my eyebrows. 'What's your charity turning down?'

'Vaccines that are almost at the use by date. A woman representing the pharmaceutical giants wanted to flog these vaccines to us. And when I said no, she was willing to give them away for free.' She scrunches her forehead. 'What's that all about?'

I smile. Maybe another time I will tell her about that scam. 'How are you?'

'I'm keeping busy,' she says bravely, as two large tears roll down her face.

I wipe them away with my thumbs. 'Good. You keep busy. Is Billie coming over?'

'Yes, she'll be here at ten.'

'Good.'

'So you're off to see Jay.'

'Yes. I'll call you after and let you know what's going on.'

'Could it be a trick?'

'I don't think so.'

'Oh, my darling, I love you so much.'

'Wait for my phone call.'

'Always.'

I kiss her on the forehead, breathe in the scent of her, to fortify me on the most difficult day of my life.

The meeting with Jay is over quickly. Obviously, he thinks I've taken leave of my senses—it is in every 'uh', 'um' and uncomprehending pause that finds its way into his sentences. But he is too discreet to come right out and say it. I leave his office clutching copies of the papers Victoria requested. Copies of Sorab's return, copies of my freedom from the world I somehow became trapped in. I feel a flicker of excitement inside me, but I hold back.

Too much can still go wrong.

I get outside on the street and a long black limousine with heavily tinted windows stops in front of me. The back door closest to me opens. I am not afraid of death. I never have been. I'll do what I have to do to keep my family safe. I bend down, look inside, take a deep breath, and get into it.

'Monfort,' I state quietly.

'And what should I call you?' he asks tonelessly.

'Hopefully, you won't see me again, and that will be a moot question.'

He smiles. In the daylight his skin is particularly repulsive. White and translucent, the veins grass green. Like the damp underside of a frog.

'But you will see me again.'

'After today I'm finished.'

'I'm afraid your services are still required. Stepping off the train is a dangerous business.'

I look at my platinum Greubel Forsey Tourbillion, acquired for a cool half a million dollars at Christie's Important Watches auction two autumns ago. I take it off and place the timepiece on the console between Monfort and me. To anybody not in the know the gesture is meaningless, but to the true insider and the practitioner of dark esoteric energy, he will understand it perfectly. The gesture is unmistakable.

Then I get out of the car, close the door, and begin to walk in the opposite direction. Ten yards away Brian makes a U-turn and stops beside me. I get in.

'Take me to that bitch,' I say.

# Twenty-Nine
## Blake Law Barrington

I turn away from the window when I hear her come in. Not fast. Slowly. This is the last part. I am almost free. The lock on the chain is about to break.

The door closes behind her. She is dressed in a black and white suit, and her trademark black pearls encircle her throat. Her hair is shining and loose around her shoulders. Our eyes meet. It is impossible to think of her as anything else but my greatest enemy.

I hold out my phone.

She doesn't say a word. Looks at the papers I have spread out on the plastic table, and takes the phone from me. Our fingers don't touch.

She dials, waits for the connection and says just three words: 'The Speculative Woman.' Then she ends the call and puts it down on the table between us. I sit and so does she. Neither of us says anything. After a while she picks up the papers that are on the table and casually, as if they are a magazine that she does not care too much for, glances through them.

I turn my head and look outside. It is a beautiful day. The sun is shining. I am so tense I feel the tension inside my body wanting to manifest in some physical way. I take shallow breaths and control myself. The only sounds are of her flipping uninterestedly through the papers. After a while even she cannot be bothered to fake interest in them. She tosses them on the table and looks in my direction. I don't turn to look at her so she, too, turns her head and looks out of the window

Twenty minutes later my phone rings. My heart is thudding so loud she can probably hear it. I pick it up and Brian says, 'We got him.'

'Thanks,' I say, my voice sounding thick and guttural. For the first time since Brian called to say that Sorab had been kidnapped that lump of ice in my chest melts.

I look up at her. She is watching me curiously. As if I am an oddity she cannot understand. Or she is a child. The look unnerves me. I have arranged for her to be murdered. She is my sister.

'Siblings used to kill each other for power and inheritance,' she says.

'I don't want anything from your father. It's all yours.'

'Sometimes siblings just want revenge.'

'Is that what you want, Victoria?'

'I did.'

'What's changed?'

'You have friends in high places.'

Surprised, I stare at her. 'What are you talking about?'

'You didn't know, did you?'

'Know what?' I can feel the tension coming back into my body.

'They are not done with you.' And she smiles. A cruel taunting smile. 'You can't ride off into the sunset just yet, Blake.'

I stand. 'Are you ready to go?'

'What do you think?'

'Let's go then.'

She takes the papers on the desk and I ring the bell.

The nurse comes and opens the door. We walk to the reception desk. The doctor is hovering about waiting for us. I nod at him. He nods back and smiles at Victoria. She smiles back and then we are walking out into the sunshine.

Victoria lifts her face toward the sun and breathes a sigh of satisfaction.

I look at her. She is my sister. The thought is foreign. I can't murder her.

She turns and looks at me. 'If she had not come we would have mated and bred. And produced something special.'

I shudder inwardly. 'We might have produced monsters.'

She smiles. 'You don't understand. That's what they want.'

A hired chauffeured Bentley comes to a stop at the bottom of the steps. 'Here's your ride. Goodbye, Victoria.'

She shrugs and walks down the rest of the steps and gets smoothly into the back of the car. The driver closes the door and tips his head toward me before he drives off. For a moment I stand on the steps and lift my face toward the warm rays of the sun as Victoria had done. I can't do it. I can't kill another person in cold blood.

I take out my mobile and call him. He picks up the call, but does not say anything.

'Abort the plan. Do you understand?'

'Yes. Plan aborted,' the voice on the other side says quietly.

My breath comes out in a great rush of relief, 'Thank you.'

I feel a sudden shift inside me, a strange letting go. All the actions that have brought me to this moment have been sanctioned by a higher power than their demonic God. He did not win. Never once in my nightmares did the horse manage to break down the flimsiest of wooden doors and come to me. And never again would he be able to.

I will take my little family and go where no one knows us.

# Victoria Jane Montgomery

I get into the car and watch him through the window. How very strange. The voices in my head have all fallen totally silent. Could it be that I have left them all behind in that wretched place? I watch Blake's large, lightly tanned manly hand close the door—I've always loved his hands—and a single tear rolls down from one eye. I touch it and look at it with amazement.

I must still love him... Shame he will be dead soon.

A twinge of something hurts my heart, but I will not meddle with it. It will make a sniveling, timorous coward out of me.

The car pulls away, and I turn back to look at him through the back window. Framed against the hospital he stands very still. Seems such a waste. Such a contradiction to kill that which you love so deeply. Such a beautiful man, too. But I'd rather stand by his grave, below a hill, where a sentinel Cyprus tree stands guard and mourn a loss love than watch her victorious.

'Where are you taking me?' I ask the driver.

'Longclere Hall, Lady Victoria,' he replies politely.

It will be good to see my parents again. I sit back and cannot help smiling. I'm out and I'm free. I look down at the papers in my hands. I did it. I crushed him and next I will crush her. But her death will not come easy. I will make her beg me to die. I turn my head to look out of the window and my smile freezes. A tall, souped up SUV with large metal guards is speeding towards us. They planned it well. They knew which side I'd be sitting in. As it crashes into the side of the Bentley with a sickening sound of crushing metal, and a white hot pain, my gasp simmers in the air.

Once, a long time ago, I had a laugh like the tinkling of chandelier glass. A sweet sound. It's not lost. There it is in the distance, but coming nearer. The light gets brighter and whiter than anything I have ever seen.

It's a relief to let go.

# Thirty
## Blake Law Barrington

Our highest truths are but half-truths; think not to settle down forever in any truth. Make use of it as a tent in which to pass a summer's night, but build no house of it, or it will be your tomb.

—Earl Balfour

I watch the car bearing Victoria move away from me until it turns the corner at the driveway and disappears from view. Across the road Tom is waiting for me. I take a step toward him, and I see a long black limousine, its windows tinted black, crawling toward me. I am not afraid to die, I never have been. It comes to a stop beside me. I lift my face toward Tom, let him know that all is fine. Perhaps I won't be long, but even if I am, all is fine. I did the right thing. No more will I bloody my sword.

I open the door and a blast of air-conditioned, gently perfumed air hits me in the face. The perfume is disconcertingly familiar. Sick to my stomach, I bend my neck and look into the dim interior.

'Hello, Blake,' my mother says.

I look at her with dazed eyes. In the rubbish and the flotsam of the memories discarded as unimportant, tiny events, little snippets of conversations, a look here, a gesture there, bubble to the top and demand recognition. Delicate nuances of a language I did not understand until now. The darkened cold interior of the car yawns. I fall into it, feeling sick to my stomach, and close the door with a soft click.

'I killed the wrong parent, didn't I?'

She smiles. 'You killed the right parent. You just didn't kill the power behind the throne.'

'You?'

'Your father, as powerful as he was, was nothing more than the visible, coarser grains in the suspension of particles that is this war in our matterium. Power is never where you think it is, and never kept where one can see it. The value of anonymity for continuous power is incalculable. If you see something then you can reach out and take it.'

I stare at her with astonishment. I could not have been more amazed or shocked if she had grown horns. Nobody could ever have imagined that behind the scenes she is the hidden hand. The invisible power in the grand scheme of things. It is impossible for me to describe what I feel. Even the thought that my own mother is one of a handful of the most powerful people in the world, known only to the highest initiates, sitting at the pinnacle of the pyramid of world domination and directing the agenda of all the secret societies in the world, is too fantastical to believe. And yet here she is.

'Why are you here?' I ask, dazed.

'Your car is due for an accident.'

'I canceled the hit on Victoria,' I say dully.

'We did not.' She glances at her watch. 'It should have been done by now.'

'Why?'

'Because her plan was to kill my son, then my grandson, and finally my dead son's wife.'

I am transfixed by her haughty, magisterial eyes. Something flashes into my mind, something indefinable. Fuck, there is just no escape. No matter which way I turn, how far I run, I always end up at the same door. I turn away from her and press my palms into my eyes. Oh, Victoria, Victoria! It seems you will have your revenge, after all.

'Would you like some iced tea?' my mother offers kindly.

'No,' I say, slowly. I take my palms away from my eyes and face her. 'And what do you want in exchange?'

'A successor. A hidden hand to hold the power after me.'

'Me?'

She shakes her head slowly. 'It was never you.'

Something inside me shrivels and dies quietly, but my voice remains calm and distant. 'Why not one of Marcus's sons?'

She shakes her head again. 'The die was cast. By you.'

'No,' I state firmly. 'You can't have Sorab.'

'He is not yours to give. Children come through us but they do not belong to us. The decision to join us is his to make.'

'He won't join you. I will teach him different from what I was taught. I will bring him up to know right from wrong.'

She nods as if conceding. 'By all means. You may educate him in any way you wish, but if he decides, when he is able to, to join us, you must not stand in his way. That is all I ask.'

'Why would he ever want to join a brotherhood of death and destruction if he had choice?'

'You have your role to play. I have mine. He has his.'

'And if I agree, you will leave my family alone.'

'Until Sorab is eighteen, we will never contact him.'

'What will you do? Trap him into committing some crime or scandal and then blackmail him?'

'No. That won't be necessary.'

I frown. 'Offer him money, power and prestige?'

She seems amused. 'Sorab is a catalyst. Offering him such things would be a waste of time.'

'What then?' I ask, frustrated.

'I'm afraid I can't tell you more.'

'Thanks, *Mother*.'

She smiles gently. 'It's all a beautiful and intricate game. Be courageous in the path you have chosen. There is nothing to fear. You have within yourself all that you wish to become and much more that you cannot yet even imagine. May our infinite creator bless and guide your path.'

I can hardly recognize her. I have only ever known her for malicious wit and vicious gossip, the spoilt wife of an astoundingly rich man, the unrivaled queen of the Kingdom of Snobbery. The transformation is too great to comprehend. 'Why have you chosen the path you have?'

She looks at me as if I was a child again. I can barely remember her like this. Perhaps one little memory when I was five survives the brutality of my upbringing.

'I was born into it. We are obliged. It is our divine destiny and we play the part given to us by our creator. We help prepare the harvest, by separating the wheat from the chaff, for want of a more eloquent metaphor. If there were no protagonists in this world, there would be no opportunity for a human soul to choose 'good' over 'evil'. The negativity we perpetuate is a tool. Everything is a tool. This conversation is a tool. Use it as such.'

'But the wars, the wanton destruction of water, air and earth—where is the choice there?' I ask.

'We are the hidden hands. Our job is to provide the catalyst. Yours is to use it. Violence, war, hatred, green control, enslavement, genocide, torture, moral degradation, prostitution, drugs— all these things and more, they serve our purpose. What do you do in relation to our urgings? Will you succumb to the darkness or will you stand and shine your inner light? If I put a gun in your hand, I am giving you a tool. It has the potential to be either positive or negative. The outcome depends on you.'

I drop my face into my hands. My heart feels so heavy.

'Remember always that it is just a game. No one really gets hurt or dies. Offstage we are all the best of friends.'

I turn on her angrily. 'Dress it up all you want. I don't want Sorab to play catalyst. I want him to have a normal life.'

'Can you look beyond what your eyes are showing you? Express love and happiness in a world of fear and darkness, and if you can, you will be as a beacon of light into the darkness.'

I look at her. 'All right. I take up your challenge. We'll see who gets Sorab.'

'Goodbye, Blake.'

She presses a button and the car comes to a stop. I get out and close the door and the car moves away.

# Thirty-One
## Lana Barrington

How can I describe that moment Brian brought Sorab back to me? I had been told to stay indoors, and I was standing at the window that looks out to the gate when I saw them. Oh! I wanted to cry or call out to Sorab, but I couldn't. I was so happy I lost my voice. There was not a word I could say. I turned around and ran to the front door. And it was Sorab who spoke first.

'Mummy,' he said.

I burst into tears. I couldn't help it. I grabbed him from Brian and squeezed him so hard he squealed. Then he held onto my neck and said, 'Sorab home.'

'Oh, darling. Yes, you are. You are home.'

He waved at our housekeeper and he blew Geraldine a shy flying kiss but he wouldn't leave me. I wouldn't have let him go to anyone else anyway. I took him inside and he was hungry, poor thing. We made him scrambled eggs and a slice of toast and afterwards I let him have a red lollipop. I was so happy but all the time I kept glancing at the phone.

Finally, Blake calls to say he is on his way home. His voice trembles with emotion.

'Are you happy, Lana?'

'Yes, I'm happy.'

'Good,' he says softly.

'Is everything all right, Blake?'

'Yes, everything is just fine.'

And I laugh, a shaky, nervous, overjoyed sound. I feel as if we are just starting again. We've been given a second chance.

'Say hello to Sorab,' I say and hold the phone to his ear. I don't know what he says, but Sorab listens intently and suddenly grins.

I am still holding Sorab pressed against my body when our housekeeper comes in with a slim black box.

'Someone dropped this off at the front gate,' she tells me.

I take the box from her curiously, snap it open and frown.

Inside, nestled on velvet, is Blake's watch.

## Epilogue

'Time and the ocean and some guiding star and High Cabal have made us what we are.'
—Sir Winston Churchill,
Prime Minister, UK, 1940–1945 & 1951–1955

The woman awakens to the sound of a child's laughter floating in through the open windows. She smiles and stretches, then strokes her belly. It is just beginning to show. A very small bump. She sits up and, hooking her feet into slippers, goes to the window. She can see her husband and son at the bottom of the garden. The boy is perched on his father's shoulders and trying to peer into a bird's nest.

She has the urge to run to them, but she doesn't. Instead she savors that scene, a moment of beauty and joy. We have survived something so profound that it has bound us together like a tightly woven rope, she thinks. We aren't the same fun-loving innocent people we once were but we are finally free.

Suddenly overwhelmed by emotion she finds herself running out of the bedroom and down the stairs like a child. Hurtling towards them.

 192

At the double doors that lead to the garden she takes off her slippers and steps lightly on the tiles. They are already sun warmed. It is a beautiful day and there is not a cloud in the sky. The grass is cool under her feet. Before the man or the child have realized, she is already there. She throws her arms tightly around his waist and lays her cheek against his warm shirt. He stumbles forwards slightly with surprise and her son squeals. 'Oh, Mummy,' he scolds, 'you're going to make Daddy and I fall down.'

'Daddy and me,' she corrects automatically.

Her husband doesn't say anything, just looks down indulgently at her.

'What are the two of you doing?'

'We're looking at bird's eggs, but we're not allowed to touch them.'

'That's it,' her husband says and puts the boy on the ground. Then he turns around fully to look at her. 'Hey, gorgeous,' he says to her.

'You have no idea how often I dreamed of this day,' she says.

'Look, Daddy. I found a beetle,' the boy cries and holds out his cupped palms.

'Be careful, Sorab,' his father warns. 'You don't want to kill it. Even the lowly beetle's life is precious to it.'

The woman raises her eyebrow. 'Don't you think it's a bit early for philosophy lessons?'

'No,' says the man. 'It's never too early for him to learn wrong from right.'

'But Mummy kills ants all the time,' the boy says.

'Well,' sighs the man. 'Mummy only kills them when they come into the house and make a nuisance of themselves.'

The boy opens his hand and the beetle flies out of it. He begins to run after it and the man turns to his woman.

'Do you ever miss that other life, Blake?'

'Never,' he states emphatically.

'Nothing at all?'

He lays his hand on his wife's belly and spreads his fingers out. 'You are more beautiful to me today than ever.'

'Answer the question,' she teases.

He looks into her eyes and makes a mental note of their color, how it has deepened with her pregnancy. 'Oh Lana, Lana, Lana,' he sighs softly. 'When I met you, my heart was a blank canvas. Now, it is a kaleidoscope of color, rich and eternal.'

She smiles and lets his words warm her insides.

This is just the beginning...

Because this is a totally reader-generated effort
–

here is another constant reader request.

# POV

## Blake Law Barrington

### When Lana Returned Home After Kissing Jack

She opens the front door of the apartment and finds me standing in the corridor. She stops and stares at me. I know her so well I can almost read her thoughts. *Why is he home? Why is he looking at me like that?* It's a funny thing, but that look of surprise—For fuck's sake, she has no idea at all what she is doing to me—totally flips my switch. And I start to move. Without thinking.

Without control!

In a flash, I have crossed the room and closed the door. I watch myself bend my head to kiss her and then rear back as if burned. Fuck her. She really does carry his scent, too. I want to strangle him. How dare he? How dare she? My eyes blaze into hers. She looks at me as if I am a maniac. Then I really lose it. Things happen so fast it's a blur. I grab her by the upper arms and the next moment I have lifted her off the ground and she is lying dazed. Yup, flat on her back with me crouching over her like a fucking beast. I pull her skirt up and tear her underwear with my bare hands. Then I grab her legs by the kneecaps and open them wide. I jerk my face between her legs, and like a dog I *sniff* her pussy. The scent is sweet and familiar. My first reaction is to lick her and fucking take her right there. Stamp her with the scent of my possession. But I realize that I am holding onto legs that have been shocked into total stillness.

When I raise my head and look at her she is staring at me, speechless with disbelief and horror. Suddenly she seems to find her strength, and raising herself on her elbows, she stamps her feet on the carpet and pushes hard and away from me. I grab her foot and she kicks out with the other. I grab that one too and pull her toward me. She slides helplessly along the carpet, like a rag doll toward me. Her hands flail.

'Don't,' I growl. 'I smelt a man on you.'

She stops fighting. When her face is very close to mine she closes her eyes. 'I kissed Jack.'

That cuts me. I take a sharp breath. 'Why?'

She opens her eyes and stares at me. 'Because he is leaving for a war-torn country. Because I may never see him again. Because he asked me and he has never asked me for anything before,' she sobs. Tears flow freely. I have never been able to resist her tears.

I scoop her up in my arms 'Shh... I'm sorry, I'm sorry. I didn't mean to frighten you,' I croon.

But I cannot make her stop. The tears run quickly down her temples.

'Please don't cry. You didn't do anything wrong. I just can't bear thinking of you with anyone else. I don't even want you in the same room with other men,' I confess.

'What is happening to us, Blake?' she whispers. She sounds scared. I have frightened her with my aggression.

'Nothing is happening to us. I just lost my head for a moment. I didn't think. It was pure instinct.'

'What's going to happen when the forty-two days are up, Blake?'

Not that again. I can't tell her anything. Even what I have just done is incriminating. He will know when he sees the tapes that she is special. He will see me lose control. I will simply have to be more careful from now on.

'I don't know,' I tell her, 'but will you trust me that everything I do is in your best interests?'

'And what is in my best interests, Blake?'

I can see that it is tearing her up inside. My heart feels heavy. How I wish I could tell her? But I can't. Too risky. Strange, how much I want to tell her. I've never wanted to make another human being happy before. 'In thirty-one days you will know.'

Gently, I start kissing her eyelids, her cheeks that still smell of him and her mouth. I kiss her hard, force her lips open and thrust my tongue into her mouth, making her suck my tongue. Possessively, staking claim on what is mine, erasing the mark, even the memory of his mouth. My hands unbutton her blouse, cup her breasts. She lets me lift her so I can undo her bra clasp. I pull the blouse out of her skirt. It slips easily from her shoulders. The skirt follows.

I claim her on the floor beside the front door.

To anyone watching or listening let it be known: this is *my* woman.

Hey you awesome ☺ people,

Sadly, we have reached the end of the Lana and Blake story. When I began this journey back in the autumn of 2013, I had no idea where it might lead, not even if I would still be writing books one year on.

It was always my hope that my readers would find the characters of Lana and Blake endearing, but never did I imagine they would have such a strong connection with you. I am truly humbled by your loyalty to this series and for all your reviews, emails, and words of encouragement thank you from the bottom of my heart. You are like my dear friends now and for you I am writing something new.

Below are my forthcoming releases. Until the back of the next book I wish your life to be filled with great stories and unforgettable characters.

Big, big kiss to all...

*Georgia*

Love is
deceptive...

# Masquerade

Amazon # 1 Best Selling Author
## ·GEORGIA LE CARRE·

# One

## Billie Black

'Fucking kids,' I swear and bury my head under the pillow, but the irritating ringing of the doorbell continues mercilessly. The desire to go out and throttle them is so strong it makes me grit my teeth.

I pull myself out from under my pillow abruptly with a frown. Hang on a minute. I no longer live in the poor end of Kilburn, and there are no kids roaming the corridors annoying people on Sundays here. Also, I have no debts left so it can't be debt collectors either. Not that those lazy fuckers will work on Sundays.

I get out of bed and, walking barefoot to the front door, curiously put my eye to the spy hole.

Whoa!

I draw back hastily, and press my hand to my shocked belly. This is far worse than any debt collector. By far worse. The bell rings again and holds. The sound is loud and insistent. It's not going to go away. I turn my head and look at myself in the mirror on the wall. My hair is a spiky rat's nest. I pull my fingers viciously through the

unruly mess, but it does not improve. The bell goes again. Oh, fuck it! Whatever. I don't care, anyway. I take a deep breath, rearrange my face into one of impatient exasperation and fling open the door.

Cor... Look at that. Tight black T-shirt packed hard with muscles, he fills the corridor like the Incredible Hulk, only he is all blond, and he makes little kitty clench tight even on a Sunday. Damn this man to hell. How can anyone look this good at this time of the morning?

He removes his finger coolly off my doorbell and smiles a devastatingly attractive smile, before letting his gaze, all wicked and sexy, start roving down my body. It's like having melted chocolate poured all over me. I want to lick myself. Keep it together now.

'What do you want?' I demand aggressively.

'To fuck you senseless.'

I don't succeed in stifling the gasp that rises into my mouth. The cheek of the man is astounding. Last night he brazenly introduces me to his girlfriend, and this morning he stands on my doorstep wanting a legover! I feel a fine rage in my veins.

'Fuck off, you cheating skunk,' would, as Ali down the sweet shop would say, be giving him too much face. 'Piss off, I don't want you to fuck me senseless,' would be a lie. So: I nod, and move quickly to slam the door in his lazily smiling face. With lightning speed he lays his palm firmly against the wood and resolutely pushes his way in. I am engulfed by the smell of his freshly showered body. Probably washing off her smell, I think sourly. I don't do the undignified thing and attempt to fight against such a male show of strength. I will decimate him with pithy wit instead.

Inside, he looks as out of place as a rhino in a China shop.

'The polite thing to do would be to offer me some tea,' he says, one blond eyebrow arching.

I cross my arms over my chest. 'I'm actually not feeling very polite at the moment.'

He flashes a pearly white grin: wolfish in the extreme. The guy is a walking sex bomb. 'That's just grand,' he says. 'We can be impolite together.'

Pithy wit deserts me. 'Don't make me punch you in the face.'

'You were the best lay I ever had.'

My eyes widen. The surge of pleasure I experience irritates me. I pretend to laugh dryly. 'Is that supposed to be some sort of compliment?'

'Yeah, and a goddamn fine one too.'

Before we go any further, let me first tell you that this man is good in bed. And I mean he's really, really good. Like out of this world good. He butterflyed my legs and went to work on my girly bits with the precise dedication of a Swiss watchmaker until I nearly fainted with pleasure. And believe me, I'm the expert in muff diving, since I have been for most of my life a lesbian.

'Well, you were the worst lay I ever had,' I lie.

Unoffended, he laughs merrily. 'Time to make amends, then.'

'Don't you fucking dare come near me,' I warn. I realize instantly that there is not enough threat and too much desperation in my voice.

His eyes glint, dark and dirty. They make me horribly uneasy. I'm not in charge here. We stare at each other and the rush of sexual heat that sweeps over my body makes me feel oddly dizzy. The memory of his touch still burns in my bones. Unable to speak I stare foolishly at him. The truth is I'm pissed off with this guy for not calling after he promised to, for making me sleep with my phone for nearly a month, for confusing the hell out of my sexuality, and for having a girlfriend who is the exact opposite of me, but as the seconds pass, I am not sure anymore if I am more pissed off with him or with myself for being so pathetic.

The problem is that my pulse is racing and I can't think past the aching throb between my legs. I take slow breaths as my body, the hyperaware Judas, remembers and replays the sensation of all the hard planes, the raw silk of his skin, and the absolute perfection of that one night we shared.

I blink. Big mistake.

He advances, his lips twitching with amusement.

I step backwards, purely instinctive, and he takes another step, and so do I, but in the opposite direction. A warm flush spreads over my skin. All kinds of thoughts are running through my brain.

Uppermost: of course he's going to get what he came for. I can already feel his hand on my hips, and the lure of a seriously explosive orgasm. He got me the last time through the same fearlessness of consequences he is exhibiting now. No fear of rejection. Such naked confidence can be mind-numbingly seductive.

He turned my no into a maybe and my maybe into a yes.

And afterwards, when the curiosity and desire had been aroused inside me, he delivered big. I mean BIG. I told myself that I had gone with him because I loved that he did not have a prejudged idea of beauty. He found my spider tattoos beautiful! But the truth was/is, he intrigues me like no other. My body is already craving it. It's only sex, Billie, I tell myself.

I stop retreating when I feel the hard edge of the table against my buttocks. He takes his next step silently. With his hands around my neck he tilts my face upwards and swoops down on my mouth. Sweet mother, Mary. So bad, and so hot. My will is slipping away. What will? It's been a long time. A long time. Bloody hell. He tastes so fuckin' good I want to eat him. I get lost in the raving desire that comes in waves from his mouth into mine.

For a few more pulse-ripping seconds his lips bruise mine, a clash of teeth and lips and tongues. It is brutal, arousing, and totally feral. And then I tear my mouth off. The insides of my mouth are still stinging. He is strong, I'll give him that. Very fucking strong. And that arrogant tilt to his chin. Like he should be in a vampire movie. Like he's never heard the word no.

'So you don't think I'm cute?'

'If you like psychos.'

He grins and lifts me up by the waist as if I am a doll and deposits me on the table. My legs dangle off the edge. With both his hands he rips open my nightshirt. The tearing sound is deliciously erotic. Nobody has done this to me before. Underneath I am butt naked. His eyes drop to my breasts. With a slow smile he cups them in his hands.

'I wasn't wrong last night: you've had them done,' he growls and pushes his tongue into my mouth. The man's an animal and I love it.

His tongue drives in as I suck it enthusiastically. So different from a woman's tongue. So demanding. So muscular. Suddenly his mouth leaves mine, and a complaining mewl escapes me. Watching me like a hawk he bends down to take a nipple in his mouth and sucks at it cruelly. I close my eyes and moan. His hands move lower. He spreads his fingers into the thatch of light brown curls.

'A hairy girl is hard to come by these days,' he murmurs. 'You're one in a million, Billie.'

'Fuck you.'

He runs his fingers along the slit. I am embarrassingly soaking wet for him. One finger dips inside.

'Yes,' I gasp. Even that one word sounds incoherent. I want more.

He plunders my mouth. Slowly the finger inside me becomes two and then three. The stretch is delicious, but I want more. I need more. And holy fucking shit, I know where there is smoking more. I reach for his belt.

'You're throbbing for release,' he whispers huskily as he pulls away from me and splays my legs open. He watches me, his heavy-lidded eyes roaming my thrown back throat, my excited nipples, my legs spread so wide he has a full view of my pussy dripping and swollen for him.

He tears open the condom foil and then unbuttons the top button of his bulging jeans. The zip comes down and he takes out his cock. This is the thing about us lesbians. We're used to big toys, but this boy's toy—it struts right out at a right angle to his body. In its own way it is an aggressive angry thing with large veins. I'm not really sure if I consider it attractive. Certainly it is not pretty the way a pussy is, but there is something wild about it. Something animalistic and caveman-like.

I watch while he sheathes it and obligingly open my legs wider when he plunges the raincoated thing straight into me. That scream. It came from my mouth! His large strong hands are underneath my bum tilting me upwards. Whoa...this is an attack! I wrap my legs around him and he fucks me like a wild man, furious.

We are a violent, hot tangle. I writhe and claw at him, but he rams into me until I come, quick and hard. The world shatters beautifully and becomes more perfect than before. Almost immediately he does too with a growl and expletives. Fucking like this exposes the darkest part of the soul. I bet his girlfriend doesn't see this.

I grasp the firm globes of his buttocks. We are both panting hard. We have sinned. Now that I am sated I am back to my rather inelegant situation.

'And you thought you were a lesbian,' he says with such a smug smile that I slap him, so hard his head jerks back.

'That's the first time...' he mutters.

I raise a disbelieving eyebrow.

'I've been slapped by a woman while I'm still inside her.'

I use both my hands to push him away from me, but I might as well have been pushing at a brick wall. The hands cupping my buttocks are like steel manacles.

'You've had your fun. Now get out of my home,' I force between clenched teeth.

'I'm still horny.'

I tingle at the promise his words hold. I glare at him. 'We all have our afflictions and addictions.'

Suddenly I have the fierce and surprising urge to mark him. To let her know that he has been with me. I want to claim him and then I forget about it when he sucks my tongue into his mouth. Too urgent to be gentle. Then his mouth moves, warm and wet against the side of my neck. I know what he's doing. He's sucking on my tattoos, on the blue spiders. He takes his mouth away and looks at them.

'How did you find me?' I ask.

'Not easily,' he confesses. 'I had to shell out a thousand quid. Must be nice not paying your own bills.'

I ignore the jibe. I'm not about to explain anything to him. 'What happened to last night's posh and world-weary murmur?'

He grins.

'When I first met you, you had a BBC accent. Last night it was decidedly posh and today a trace of Australian has slithered in. Will the real Jaron Rose please stand up?'

'This is the real Jaron Rose.'

'Are you going to fucking get your dick out of me?'

'I will but first let me tell you what you're going to be doing tomorrow. At three thirty p.m. sharp you will bend over this table, your elbows and hands and cheek pressed against the glass, your ass in the air barely covered by lace and transparent material. You will be wearing thongs. The rims will become soaked very quickly and you will consider using your sweating hands to masturbate to relieve the ache, but you will not. You will keep that position, nipples and cunt tingling, and wait. The high heels you'll be wearing will make your calves cramp, but you will ignore it.'

My mouth drops open.

He ignores it. 'At four I will turn up. You will not turn around to look at me or speak to me. No matter how wide your legs are I will have to correct the position by kicking apart your legs and flipping the last bit of covering over your back, so your ass is totally exposed to me. I will roughly rub your panties, find the jellied part, and dig my fingers into it. You will immediately raise your hips higher to try to catch more of my flesh, and moan the way you would if you were begging for it.

'I'll tell you to be quiet. That you are not to make a sound until I allow it. I will flick your clit through the material and your body will start bucking and squirming. At that moment I will swat your butt on the fleshiest part of your buttocks just once, but hard. My fingers might strike your clit. It will make your head spin and you are bound to cry out from the surprise of my assault. So I will spank you again. Just to hear you cry out and see the blush spread. And again, until you are panting and dripping onto my hand. Excitement, shame, joy.

'Then I will back off, make myself a cup of tea and drink it while I stare at your reddened ass ripe for the picking. Once I have had my tea I will undress. Slowly. You will strain to hear buttons, material scraping my skin, shoes sliding away, socks pulling, zip tearing. I will grasp the reddened, burning skin in my palms and feel its weight in my bare hands.'

I try not to show it but his dick is slowly growing inside me and I am starting to want him to fuck me all over again.

'Then I will pull the warm red cheeks apart and holding them apart with one hand I will slide my finger into you, first one, then two and eventually three. You will moan, and shiver and maybe even grunt like an animal. Your head will start to lift off the table—you are about to come. That is the moment I'll stop and will ask you to touch yourself. You will take your hand off the table and press it between your legs, turning your head to look at me while starting to masturbate.

'"Do you want my cock in your pussy?" I will ask. "Yes," you will whisper. I will ask you again. "Yes, yes," you will plead.

'And that is when I will ram so hard into you, you will shudder and scream and arch and quiver and come in a screaming rush.'

'I won't be in at three thirty p.m. or four p.m. tomorrow,' I tell him proudly.

'Don't be absurd. Of course you will.'

'If I am bent over the table, who will let you in through the front door?'

'That's my affair. You just assume your position.'

He pulls out of me. And fully erect he takes a step away from me. I close my legs and slip off the table. Expertly, he removes the condom. I watch him pull his underpants up and over the rigid flesh.

'It won't break, will it?'

 212

He laughs and pulls his jeans over the bulge. 'Concern from you is always nice.'

'Don't mistake curiosity for concern.'

He zips up. 'See you at four.'

I don't say anything, simply stare at him.

# *Two*

When the door closes behind him my breath comes out in a rush. Holy Moly! That was unbelievable and that was not enough. I am still throbbing with need. What is it about this guy? I simply can't seem to get enough of him. I go to the fridge and pour myself a shot of vodka. I lift it up to my lips, and put it back on the counter. I don't want to take the edge off the way I feel right now. I light a cigarette and walk onto the balcony. I blow out a smoke ring and my mobile goes.

I pick it up from the coffee table and it is my best friend, Lana.

'Hey,' I say.

'Guess where I am?' she squeals.

Well, it's Sunday. Tomorrow is a working day. Her billionaire banker husband's yacht is moored in the South of France. So the South of France would be my guess. 'No idea,' I tell her.

'The South of France.'

'Brilliant.'

'I tried to call you earlier to see if you wanted to come, but I guess you were asleep.'

'I was. So what is the little sprog up to?' I ask referring to my godson.

'He seems determined to swim across the English Channel.'

'That's my boy.'

'What are you up to?'

I kill my cigarette on the balcony railing. 'Enjoying a post-coital cigarette.'

'What?'

'Jaron came around and we had sex?'

'Really?'

'Unless I dreamed it.'

'Oh my God!'

'That's what I thought.'

'Well, go on then, tell me what happened?'

'It was hot and kind of dirty, and he wants to come around tomorrow for more, but I'm not sure how I feel about it all.'

'Why?'

'I think it's that crazy-eyed girlfriend of his. Mind you, I don't feel bad about him cheating on her. I just hate the idea of him inside her.'

'My, my, I've never seen you jealous before.'

'I'm not jealous.'

'Could have fooled me.'

'Well, he's not available. So that's the end of that story.'

'I don't know what the story is between them, but I got the impression last night that he doesn't care about her one bit. There wasn't enough heat between them to keep an egg warm. It was obvious she wanted to claim him as hers, but he only had eyes for you.'

'Well...'

The doorbell goes again.

'Hang on a minute. Someone's at the door,' I say, and walk towards it. I look through the spy hole.

'Talk of the devil,' I say.

'What?'

'Call you back.'

I look again out of the spy hole. She is dressed to the nines in a white pantsuit, a long cream coat, sunglasses and a fringe sharp enough to skin a goat. I turn to the mirror and look at myself. My hair is a mess, my nightie is torn in half, and I have that slack, just-fucked look. With a grin I open the door.

**Coming soon...**

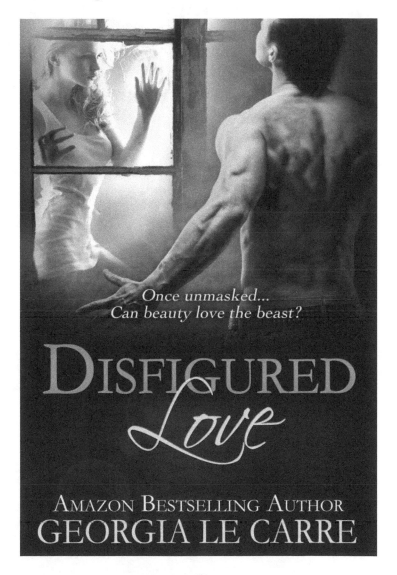

*Once unmasked...*
*Can beauty love the beast?*

# DISFIGURED
## Love

AMAZON BESTSELLING AUTHOR
# GEORGIA LE CARRE

# Synopsis

# Disfigured Love

## Once unmasked, can beauty love the beast?

My name is Lena Seagull. I should still be in school, hanging out with friends, meeting boys, falling in love—just like you. But on my eighteenth birthday my father sold me. Now, those are yesterday's dreams.

My home is a remote castle. And the man who owns me? I have never seen him.

Guy Hawk keeps his face hidden under a mask. At first, I knew only fear, but now his voice and touch make me unashamedly want him. Each night, his hired help blindfolds me, and takes me to his room.

He whispers that I am beautiful and we have sex. It is wild and exciting, but when I awaken he is always gone.

He and his castle hold dark secrets that I must unravel, but what he fears most—being unmasked—is my deepest desire.

Will either of us survive the consequences of my desire?

Disfigured Love will be a full length standalone novel.

**To be released - Fall 2014.**